Meet a Rogue at Midnight

MIDNIGHT MEETINGS BOOK 4

GINA CONKLE

BOOKS FROM DRAGONBLADE PUBLISHING

Knights of Honor Series by Alexa Aston
Word of Honor
Marked By Honor
Code of Honor
Journey to Honor

Legends of Love Series by Avril Borthiry
The Wishing Well
Isolated Hearts
Sentinel

Heart of the Corsairs Series by Elizabeth Ellen Carter
Captive of the Corsairs

Also From Elizabeth Ellen Carter
Dark Heart

Knight Everlasting Series by Cassidy Cayman
Endearing

Midnight Meetings Series by Gina Conkle
Meet a Rogue at Midnight, book 4

Second Chance Series by Jessica Jefferson
Second Chance Marquess

Imperial Season Series by Mary Lancaster
Vienna Waltz
Vienna Woods
Vienna Dawn

TABLE OF CONTENTS

DEDICATION

This book is dedicated to all the grandparents out there.
You make a difference.

ACKNOWLEDGMENT

Lots of hands go into the making of a book. This novella is no exception to that rule. When I heard Kathryn Le Veque was interested in a Georgian romance, I was excited to work with her. Her vision for Dragonblade Publishing along with her dedication to helping authors has been evident from day one. From the drool-worthy cover (thank you Dar!) to the great PR from Beth and Kris to Scott Moreland keeping my story in line(!), thank you for the Dragonblade welcome. You all have done a super job.

I also want to send a big hug to my agent extraordinaire, Sarah Younger, and my assistant, Kelly Oakes, for all the fab ideas. Lastly, thank you Brian…for making lots of dinners, doing lots of dishes, and for lots of wisdom and love.

Thanks again, Dragonblade Publishing. You rock!

Chapter One

JONAS STOOD BARE-ARSE naked before a crackling fire, bathwater dripping down his chest. There was no time for a proper dry off. The drapes were stirring in his bedchamber though the window was closed. He snatched velvet breeches off the chair and slipped them on, casual as you please—minus his smalls. All his clothes sat in a battered sea chest next to a pair of black boots peeking out beneath blue drapes.

Boots that weren't his.

With a cautious hand, he lifted a heavy dragoon pistol off the mantel, keeping an eye on the modest-sized side boots. A lad? Who would want to ambush him here? His coming home to Plumtree should be of no consequence, not after ten years gone.

The village and his grandfather's stone house hadn't changed much. Humble, quaint, and cramped. He didn't belong here. Not anymore. The sooner he took care of matters with his grandfather, the Captain, the sooner he'd be on his way.

But, his first order of business was dispatching the unskilled housebreaker.

"I know you're hiding behind the curtains. Show yourself."

The boots didn't move. Howls of laughter drifted up from downstairs. Christmas Eve celebrations must be going well in the parlor. The house burst with fresh pine boughs and spiked cider, the green and spicy scents floating everywhere.

"Come now," Jonas said, buttoning his placket with the pistol in hand. "This is not a night for ill will."

Housebreaking was a serious crime with grisly consequences. He'd give the lad an earful while sneaking him out by the scruff. But, it'd have to be quick. The Captain was expecting him…all the better to convince Jonas to stay for good. Raucous guffaws exploded through the floorboards. Mr. Goodspeak, fine soul that he was, brayed the loudest. Fiddle music played a Yuletide carol in double time while salty, old sailors stomped a bad rhythm. The Captain must've shared his best whiskey, the kind that warmed a man as good as a woman.

Weary from a hard day's ride, Jonas could use a dram. And a woman.

"I'll count to three." He padded barefoot across the room, holding the dragoon against his thigh. "One…two…"

The drape bulged with the business end of a pistol. Jonas froze. This changed the complexion of things. Eyes narrowing, his finger curled over the trigger.

"…thr—" Jonas dropped low and rammed his shoulder into the housebreaker's midsection.

"*Umph!*" A shiny piece clattered to the floor. A fine Spanish wheel lock.

Jonas kicked the weapon backward. Fists pummeled his back as white hot pain shot up from his toes. He looked down at a black boot mashing his foot.

"Enough," he growled, hoisting the lad over his shoulder.

Foot throbbing, Jonas spun away from the window. Cloth ripped overhead. The drapes and rod crashed down on their heads. Whoops and hollers rang through the house. The Captain and his cronies had to be deep in their cups not to hear this scuffle. Jonas knocked the wool off his face as the housebreaker kicked and…*squealed.*

Squealed? He squinted at the bottom wiggling against his cheek, and the split second cost him. A knee jabbed his ribs.

"*Oomph!*" His gun slipped, and the brass buttcap hammered his already aching toes. Air hissing through clenched teeth, Jonas hop-stepped to the bed. "Stop!" he bellowed and landed all his weight on the lad.

The bed rattled from the assault. The housebreaker sunk into the down mattress, fighting hard. Blue drapes sheathed the fool from head to toe. Jonas drove his head into the criminal's chest and two mounds pressed his face. Soft, round, and jiggling.

He blinked, a slow smile forming. He was nose deep between sizeable breasts—an excellent pair as breasts go swathed in old drapes.

"Well, bugger me."

The housebreaker wheezed. "I'd...rather...you get off me!"

Jonas rolled sideways and clamped his thigh across her thrashing legs. The woman's mouth gaped behind wool like a caught fish. She flopped like one, too. A feminine hip squirmed at the juncture of his thighs. Fingers clawed the curtain. His midnight visitor tussled fiercely with the drape, the bed ropes creaking madly beneath her.

"*Shhh.* Let me uncover you," he said, staying her busy hands.

"So you can shoot me?"

"No. So you can breathe easy." His grip on her wrists was full of authority. "We can stay like this all night, or you can trust me. It's your choice."

Yellow firelight danced on waves of mussed bed sheets. Land-locked sailors sang off-key below stairs. Music pitched fast and high from the parlor, but the storm on his mattress calmed. Tautness in the wrists he held eased a fraction. The housebreaker lay stiffly against him, smelling oddly of...vinegar.

She panted against the drape. "You call those choices?"

"Best I can do for a woman who pointed a pistol at me."

Grumbling came from the drape. Jonas's blood pumped with satisfaction. His lush, midnight visitor was at his mercy. This homecoming wasn't so bad, not when the housebreaker's hip brushed his ballocks. He grinned, liking her pliant against him. The skirmish was over.

"Well?" she said, her body lax. "Are you going to get this off me?"

Copper-hued hair shined through a tear in the cloth. The woman in his bed was a gift trussed in blue wool, excitement in his otherwise dull Christmas Eve. It was time he unwrapped his present. He stuck a finger in the hole and yanked. Threads snapped, showing bold brown eyes staring at him through tangled hair. Ready to see the rest of her, he ripped thick cloth with both hands down to the soles of her scrubby boots.

A lovely mouth opened wide and sucked fresh air. "Thank you."

His comely housebreaker lay dressed in homespun breeches and a plain shirt open at the neck. A gentleman's faded bottle green coat flopped wide as she brushed hair off her face. Exquisite breasts free of a corset, shift, and waistcoat ruined the mannish disguise. Cambric stretched across dainty nipples at the center of curves flattened as nature would have it when a woman was on her back. The siren's chest rose and fell with alluring rhythm, the sight striking him speechless.

"Did you get your fill?" She snapped her coat shut and laughed. "Welcome home, Jonas *Bacon* Braithwaite."

SIN-BLACK HAIR WITH angelic blue eyes shouldn't be an earthly possibility, yet Jonas wore the combination as though his appeal didn't matter. Plumtree's rebel son was never one to charm the ladies; his brother Jacob owned that talent. In his youth, Jonas had muddled through conversation when the fair sex flirted with him. From farmer's daughters to highborn ladies, women were drawn to the quiet lad like flies to honey, but this man with a gold piece twinkling from his ear dripped with confidence.

Olivia sat bolt upright. "What's this?" She tapped the gold hoop. "Were you a gentleman of fortune? Possibly a *pirate?*"

His head jerked back at her familiar touch.

She smiled and braced a hand on his bed. "You don't remember me, do you?"

The notion pricked her pride. Her chin tipped higher and she waited. She'd been a girlish fourteen when Jonas last saw her, and he a strapping young man of twenty.

Eyes scrunching, he searched her face and form, a warm tingle following wherever his gaze touched.

"Livvy? Livvy Halsey?"

"In the flesh." She nodded at his well-formed chest. "And you might want to cover some of yours."

Massive arms crossed his chest, the muscled hills and trenches of those limbs earned from years of sea going adventures if the tales she'd heard were true.

"You've seen my chest before."

Oh, but not this fascinating version of Jonas. The flesh she'd seen had been when village lads held a wrestling match in her family's meadow. Battling barefoot in shirtsleeves and breeches, Jonas took all comers. Two of them attacked him at once. A boy grabbed his shirt and the fabric ripped in two.

"Explain yourself," he said. "What are you doing in my bedchamber at midnight?"

Skin on her neck flushed, the heat dancing feather-soft to her cheeks. She wasn't a child to be reprimanded. Or was it Jonas in a state of dishabille? His placket was half-fastened, and the fire's dim light touched shoulders wider and stronger than she remembered. Black curls framed brown male nipples, the discs as intriguing as the coarse black hair encircling them. Her body wanted to stay put, but her brain cried for distance.

"I, I came to get something." She slid off the mattress, her bottom brushing his bed sheets, the intimate sound seductive. The Jonas of her childhood was the heart of mild infatuation, but this man made her body sluggish and her pulse heavy. She gripped the ends of her coat, needing something to hold. Their tumble warmed her to the core, so did the view of him bathing.

She'd not timed this well at all.

"Don't play coy," he said. "Last I saw you, your braids were flying as you galloped away."

"And last I saw you, your lips were stuck to my sister."

Chuckling, he leaned back on the bed post. "How is Elspeth?"

Her fingernails dug into her coat. "She's well. Married and widowed since you've been gone."

Black brows knit together as Jonas absorbed the news. Head shaking, his blue gaze pinned her. "Sorry to hear about her loss, but you need to explain yourself."

"I think not. Years ago, I might've done your bidding like a tame puppy, but I'm not a child anymore."

His smile pinched at the corners. "I noticed."

Barks of laughter rang through the house. The Yuletide song was done, the cue for her to leave. She smiled gamely, taking a cautious side-step toward the wheel lock. Jonas must've read her intent because he was off the bed nimble as a cat, standing between her and the gun.

"Don't be stubborn, Liv. What about your mother and father? They must be worried." A subtle frown clouding his face, he focused on his half-fastened placket. "This goes beyond the pale...even for you."

Spine straight, she owned her choices. There'd been many painful ones of late. The timing aside, she didn't regret her theft. But, stealing from a dear, childhood friend—even a long absent one—wasn't easy.

Not when his gentle baritone chided her.

"You're not answering me." Jonas slipped a brass button into its red velvet hole.

Such large hands. Mouth slack, a shiver skimmed her body. Facing him, she couldn't make her tongue work. A muscle bulged in the valley between his thumb and forefinger. Long fingers skimmed his placket with a deft touch, the veins and sinew twisting under his skin. Was he as careful when touching a woman? She swallowed peculiar thickness in her throat. Jonas required answers. It'd be nice to tell him who carried the burdens at home now, but to what end? Childhood was gone, taking some of her openness with it. Jonas wasn't long for Plumtree. Better to give blithe evasions, same as she did with everyone else this year.

"My mother and father are safely abed," she said. "Where I need to be, if you'd be so kind as to forget about my being here."

"Not likely."

Ruby red velvet hugged brawny thighs. Jonas glowed with good health, his flesh brown as a roasted coffee bean. Above his placket, stomach muscles flexed with grooves and hollows. He'd seen the world and by the looks of all his gloriously sun-kissed skin, the world had seen Jonas.

She licked her lips, her boots shuffling a side-step to the window. "Come now. We always looked past each other's questionable exploits."

"As you aptly pointed out, we're not children anymore." Brows furrowing, he glanced at the door. "How did you get in here anyway?"

She tipped her head at mullioned glass. "The window by way of your oak tree."

"A grown woman climbing trees." His face split with a lovely grin. "Haven't lost your spirit, have you?"

She smiled back. Strong and quiet, Jonas was the steady one in childhood storms, even when he stirred up trouble. She was tempted to curl up by the fire and ask him to spin tales of his travels. Being with Jonas had been the best part of growing up, but reckless days following the Braithwaite brothers were long over. She had her work and her family's circumstances to consider. A raven-haired adventurer wasn't part of her path. Seizing the moment, she took quick steps to the window before the night worsened. The Spanish wheel lock would have to wait.

A long arm blocked her way. "You should leave by the front door. It's safer."

"I can't," she cried. "The Captain and his guests will see me."

"What? You break into my bedchamber at midnight and you're worried about what's proper?"

"I don't make a practice of this."

"I can tell. You're not very good at it." He flipped open his sea chest. "You haven't told me why you're here. Settling some score with the Captain?"

She held her breath when he searched the chest. Would he notice the empty leather purse? Jonas peppered her with questions, his hurried hands grabbing clothes before shutting the lid. This wasn't about the Captain. This was about Jonas. The pilfered piece was tucked in her coat pocket.

"I'll…I'll tell you before Twelfth Night ends. I promise." Her voice was strained. "Let me leave quietly. Consider it a boon to an old friend."

Jonas held his shirt aloft, his deep blue stare scalding her. Her heart thudded. Air was heavy between them as laughter exploded through the floorboards. Jonas fit the white shirt over his head, the corners of his mouth tight when his face showed again.

"It'll cost you."

His smooth baritone sent a delicate shiver across secret, feminine skin.

"You can count on me to pay my debts."

The surprise was how much she still cared for him, the unexplainable depth beyond friendship and girlish infatuation. Their lives entwined from years of scrapes and merriment. Time hadn't diminished the bond. Contrary to what she'd said, she wanted him to bid her sit by the fire and question her midnight visit. Instead, Jonas gave up easily. He quietly accepted her refusal like a man keeping polite distance, a man who couldn't involve himself in her affairs. Not anymore.

Watching him dress was personal, yet Jonas donned his clothes with a casual air. A twinge sunk in her stomach: *Had he grown comfortable dressing in the company of a woman?*

"You'll want to take that home." Jonas tipped his head at the wheel lock, his fingers flying over pearled waistcoat buttons.

She retrieved the weapon and held it up by the barrel. "I brought in case I ran into one of the Captain's friends…a woman's precaution if you will." She tucked the pistol into the back waistband of her breeches. "I am sorry I pointed it at you and for stomping your foot. I was frightened….everything went fast."

He slipped on a well-traveled boot. "You're forgiven."

Between his smile and the room's muted light, her legs refused to budge. She'd watched him shave and bathe tonight. The image of him barefoot and shirtless in travel-worn breeches as he dragged his razor across his jaw had burned into her mind.

"My friendship is true as it ever was. If you need something…" Jonas's half-hearted words trailed off.

His obligatory offer wasn't enough. A man chasing down his next adventure couldn't help her. She needed someone to stay. Plumtree's gossip claimed Jonas would be gone when Twelfth Night ended. The still packed sea chest confirmed the news.

She unlatched the window panel, and Christmas Eve bathed her face with cold air. "Thank you for understanding."

"We've shared worse scrapes," he said, donning a red velvet coat.

She held on to the window frame and hooked a leg over the ledge. "Red velvet. Dashing attire for a pirate."

"Don't climb out yet. Let me get outside to see you safely off."

He disappeared from the room. She took one last breath of his lingering scent, a spicy, foreign aroma that clung to his sheets, the air. Plumtree's quiet lad, her childhood friend, was all grown up. From downstairs, male voices overlapped with hoots of laughter through the open door. It was time to go. She swung her other leg out the second-story window. Grabbing a branch bare of leaves, she planted both feet on a lower limb and scooted toward the trunk. The climb down was easy, a matter of descending the tree's convenient symmetry. Her feet landed on the ground not far from the parlor's back window where light glowed on new fallen snow. Fiddle music whined as Jonas jogged around the corner, his breath puffing tiny clouds.

He made an imposing silhouette, his heavy black coat spanning colossal shoulders. "You were supposed to wait."

"Why?" She shook out the cloak she'd left on a shrub.

"So I could catch you if you fell." His voice caressed each word, half-amused and a touch sensual.

Her hands stilled. Eyes the shade of lapis lazuli glinted with messages she shouldn't be receiving. As a woman of twenty-four years, she was acquainted with lust. Was this shift in Jonas because he'd glimpsed her bosom tonight? He'd courted her sister, not her. Confusion swirled inside her—glee at being the object of his fancy and disappointment that her friend held the better part of himself back.

Jonas was a man after a kiss. Nothing more.

What else could she expect? He was leaving Plumtree after all.

"I'd better go." She spun around and whipped on her cloak.

Behind her, boots crunched snow and pebbles. Light snow had fallen on Plumtree, sprinkling the world clean and white. She fastened the first frog when a firm hand touched her shoulder.

"Let me help you put that on," he murmured in her ear though his voice said *let me take that off.*

Flesh pebbled across her bottom. His baritone strummed delicate nerve endings along her inner thighs. There was something solid and poetic in his voice, a combination that made no sense, yet with Jonas, it did. Eyes closed, she willed composure.

"Livvy," he whispered and her knees weakened.

Was it possible a woman could sink in a sea of lust with a childhood friend? They'd spent summers together hunting tadpoles for goodness' sake.

Big hands grasped her shoulders and turned her around. She opened her eyes and he filled her vision. Moonlight limned ink black hair not long enough to be tied in a queue. Jonas had to have shaved his head and was growing it again. And his gold earring…it winked at her.

Yes, they both had their secrets.

Inside the house, fiddle music ebbed. Silence curled as mysterious as the crisp winter air. The Captain and his friends rumbled a new song without the fiddle, their solemn voices blending for the first time.

"God rest ye merry gentlemen, let nothing you dismay…"

Jonas cracked a smile. "At least they don't sound like howling cats."

Their bodies shook with gentle laughter. She could lose herself in him, the comfort and the thrill. Jonas dipped his head, his vivid blue gaze taking her breath away. Infinite stillness lit the depths of his eyes. Her lips parted to announce she was leaving, but Jonas slipped both hands into her unbound hair, urging her close.

Her breath hitched at large, warm hands cradling her head. Gentle heat melted her. Her thighs brushed his. She wanted Jonas…his touch, his friendship…whatever morsel of happiness he could share during his short stay in Plumtree.

Her lashes drooped. The world was his spicy soap, big hands riffling her hair, and baritone whispers of, "You've grown up, Livvy…beautiful, lively…"

Carnal lips rubbed hers, softly coaxing her mouth open.

Tender, poignant messages poured through her limbs, saying *you were made for his kisses.*

His mouth opened over hers…the lusty shock of it. She gripped his coat, fisting the wool. Her lips parted for Jonas, and the world was unsteady.

Plumtree's rebel son tasted of sharp cider and sweet, sensual promises. He teased her, his tongue skimming her lower lip before slipping into her mouth. Her body swayed into him. Their kiss deepened, and her tongue touched him back. Tremors rocked her from head to foot from the long, intimate kiss. Wet heat shot anew between her legs, but the strongest ache banged inside her heart.

Kissing Jonas was a sampling of life as it was meant to be. Vibrant. Complete. Perfect.

His mouth on hers was an invitation.

And she was ready to say yes.

Chapter Two

"ROSE PETAL JAM sets the soul right." The Captain passed off the basket to Mrs. Addington.

The lank-limbed housekeeper hugged the basket brimming with shiny jars, her ancient stare severe under her mobcap. "You will not be putting this in my Christmas box, sir. Mind you, I enjoy Mrs. Halsey's jams, but I prefer you send me off with a juicy roast goose tomorrow."

Jonas's ears pricked at the mention of Livvy's mother. He'd spent the last hour staring out the back-parlor window at the Halsey Tower in the distance. From time to time, a silhouette passed by the tower's window, and smoke puffed from twin chimneys. In years past, Mr. Halsey would toil for hours in the stone turret, restoring artifacts. Roman pieces were his favorite. He'd written tomes about Rome's rule over England, all from studying ancient relics he and other antiquarians had dug up from the earth.

"Your request is duly noted, Mrs. Addington." The Captain tapped his cane twice on the floor before settling into his leather wingback chair to face Mr. Goodspeak.

The housekeeper shuffled off to the kitchen, leaving the men to their entertainments. The Captain and Mr. Goodspeak waged a battle over their chessboard, their fourth today. Mr. Meakin and Mr. Littlewood, both sat nose deep in broadsheets while Mr. Bristow snored on the rust-colored settee. The men, a mix of widowers and lifelong bachelors, had served with the Captain in the Royal Navy and were permanent fixtures in the brown and beige parlor.

Jonas leaned a shoulder against the window frame, keeping an eye on the tower window. The structure was all that remained of a centuries old castle that once sat on Halsey land. The two-story Halsey tower reminded him of Mr. Bristow on the settee—round, squat, and slumping to one side.

In the distance, two arms flung wide the tower windows and a head poked through the opening. It was near twilight, but there was no mistaking the long copper braid dangling over the windowsill. Livvy. She checked the heavens before ducking out of sight and popping up again to toss a rope out the window.

A rope?

He squinted to be sure. Yes. A rope. The thing danced like a snake as Livvy fed it hand over hand out the window.

What secrets did his midnight visitor hide in her tower?

Jonas pushed off his post. "Captain, did you say Mrs. Halsey came to call?"

"Goodness no. Her charwoman delivered the basket." The Captain nudged his rook two spaces forward. "Mrs. Halsey rarely makes social calls these days. On account of Mr. Halsey."

"Mr. Halsey?"

The Captain studied the board, his brows beetling. Mr. Goodspeak fiddled with the edge of his moustache, mulling his next move. The hearth crackled nicely and the room smelled of yesterday's pine boughs and last night's whiskey-imbued revelry. The Captain and his cronies had been slow to rise this morning, their bloodshot eyes and sluggish steps a sign of last night's fun.

"Sir?" Jonas prompted. "You were telling me about Mr. Halsey."

"Yes. Quite. All very hushed family business, I'm afraid. A matter of privacy and all that, but people talk."

"And what, pray tell, do people say?"

The Captain's age-scarred hand batted the air. "Some folderol about Mr. Halsey not being well in mind or body. It's nonsense. I saw him out for a ramble with Mrs. Halsey last summer. He walked with a cane, but so do I. And I'm fit as a fiddle."

"But not of sound mind," Mr. Goodspeak said, chortling at his own jest. "My bishop takes your rook."

The Captain frowned at Mr. Goodspeak waggling the chess piece and plucked his pipe off the mantel. "As you can see," he went on. "Light shines from his tower where he labors day and night alongside his daughter. The younger, unmarried one."

"Liv—" Jonas began before correcting himself. "You speak of Miss Olivia Halsey."

"The very same." The Captain tapped ash remnants from his pipe into the hearth and began packing it with tobacco he kept in a box on the mantel. "Strange child. Always spouting facts about aqueducts and Roman generals as I recall."

"Methinks your boy is restless," Mr. Goodspeak said. "Needs an afternoon at Plumtree's public house with more lively companionship than the lot of us."

"Here, here." Mr. Littlewood peered over the broadsheet, his bloodshot eyes owlish behind his spectacles. "Perhaps a pint and a pretty tavern maid would do." Knees cracking, his enthusiastic bulk edged forward on his seat cushion. "I'll accompany you, m'boy. Could do with a bit of conversation with a lively skirt."

"Thank you, Mr. Littlewood, but I'd rather stroll the countryside."

"A walk. In all that cold?" Mr. Littlewood's jowls shook from his distaste. "If you must. As long as our stroll takes us to the Sheep's Head—"

"Alone, if you please. I wish to walk some of my old childhood haunts." A hand behind his back, Jonas tipped his head in deference. "I wouldn't want to bore you, sir, or drag you away from all this warmth and cheer."

The Captain swiveled around in his leather chair. "Don't take long. We've much to discuss, you and I."

Jonas fisted his hand at the small of his back. How to let his grandfather down as gently as possible? He wasn't staying. The old man needed to let that dream go.

"I won't be long, sir. A walk through the plum orchard and along the canal, perhaps."

The Captain chewed his pipe, squinting at the back window, wrinkles deepening around his eyes. "Have a good stretch of the legs then."

Jonas left the parlor to don coat, hat, and gloves. Images of a dancing rope and copper braid played in his head. He exited Braithwaite cottage, the ramshackle barn bearing a sign: Braithwaite Furniture and Sons.

Except there were no sons. Only grandsons...and errant ones at that.

Fixing his collar, he beat a hasty path to his grandfather's plum orchard. Cold air dried his nostrils, and dormant grass dusted with last night's snow crunched under his boots. Years he'd trod this way with his brother, leading the village boys from one scrape after another.

The Braithwaites were Plumtree's upstarts from the beginning. The Captain, a gruff widower, had won his humble plot of land in a London card game against Mr. George Hastings. The deed in hand, Captain Braithwaite had announced that very night to fellow sailors he was giving up the sea, ready to take a turn as a furniture maker. It was the trade of the Captain's father and his father's father. But, claiming a piece of Hastings land upset Plumtree's balance of nature. A medieval king had bestowed the land on the revered Hastings family, and the Captain was a salt-tongued interloper.

Not long afterward, the old man installed his unwed daughter and her rough and tumble twin sons, Jacob and Jonas, in the Braithwaite cottage. Everyone knew the boys were born on the wrong side of the blanket.

It was years before the dust settled on *that* scandal.

Jonas pushed through the winter bare orchard, following smaller boot prints in the snow. Had to be Livvy's. She'd taken this path after sneaking out of his bedchamber last night. Livvy Halsey was a puzzle, wearing breeches and wielding a pistol. He grinned.

She'd stolen something. From him or his grandfather.

What a fine welcome home that was. Only their long childhood friendship had stopped him from sounding an alarm.

Pushing past the trees, he spied her family's tower ahead. Halsey Manor rose behind the tower, a grand garden wedged like a chessboard between the two structures. He hopped over an icy creek, his coat hem flaring around his legs. The single jump renewed him as if he stepped back in time to the agreeable parts of his youth. Of racing horses in green fields. Swimming in the River Trent. And calling on the Halsey girls to fritter away an afternoon of mischief.

He charged up the meadow's rise, his lungs bursting with rare good feeling since returning home. Livvy leaned outside the tower window, her copper braid swaying as she huffed in her struggle with the rope. A hulking wooden chair swung merrily at the end.

Cupping his mouth, he called out, "Need some help?"

Livvy's head snapped up. "Jonas? Is that you?"

He jogged to clear the ground between them, cold air biting his cheeks. Red-nosed and determined, she wrestled with rope and furniture.

He grabbed the chair and looked up. "Have a care, or you're going to fall."

A pair of lovely breasts jostled against her bodice. "I've done this many times."

"Of course you have. Doesn't every Englishwoman hang out windows and haul furniture up by rope?"

She stifled a giggle. "Don't be impertinent. You can see I'm in the middle of something."

Tufts of snow landed on his face. He made an effort to speak to her eyes, not her cleavage. "What are you doing in your tower? Spinning chairs into gold?"

"In a manner of speaking, yes, I am." She grinned at him. "You're in high spirits."

"It is Christmas Day."

"So it is." She focused on the chair and adjusted her grip on the rope. "Well, don't let me keep you from your celebrations."

She was giving him the brush-off?

He chuckled quietly against his collar. "I'm brimming with good cheer. So much that I thought I'd bring it here."

Face reddening, Livvy yanked the rope. He held the chair in place.

Her smile stuck in a stubborn line. "I don't have time to dally."

"Even with an old friend?"

He'd seen the same determination on her face years ago. She'd answered a village boy's dare and waded far into the River Trent. With her skirts waterlogged, the current had dragged her girlish frame underwater. Livvy had bobbled up and down, gasping for air. He'd dashed in after her and dragged her sputtering to the shore. Scrambling up the bank, she'd glared at him through sopping wet hair, announcing she didn't need a Braithwaite boy to save her.

Nor did she need one now.

Livvy's breath blew decisive clouds in chill air. Was her resistance about what she hid in the tower? Or him?

"Last night, you asked a boon of me when I caught you in my bedchamber. I gladly gave it. Now I ask a favor of you. Let me come in and—" he jiggled the chair "—I'll haul this up for you."

Snow thickened around his boots. Gusts swirled the flakes as if nature itself conspired to get him inside Livvy's tower.

A little give in her shoulders, a slow sigh, and, "Very well. Door's unlocked."

He trotted around the medieval tower, passing an empty hand cart by the door. Iron rivets covered the oak door painted black. He pushed past it and, ducking his head at the low ceiling, took the stone steps two at a time up the narrow, winding passage, a passage too tight for the chair's odd geometry.

Blazing light and the pungent aroma of vinegar hit him on the top floor. Four plank tables squared off the middle of the round room: each table was covered with mosaics, pottery shards, open books, jars, brushes, rags, and aged metal pieces. Three tall iron stands burned a dozen tallow candles. Two fires snapped a cheery welcome in the hearths. And one skirt-covered bottom fidgeted at the arched window.

Livvy's head bobbed up. "Hurry. My arms are getting tired."

He stepped gingerly around glossy mosaic pieces resting on canvas stretched across the floor. Settling beside her, he reached through the opening and placed his gloved hands above and below her chafed hands on the rope.

Big brown eyes fixed on him. "Have you got it?"

Livvy's side was flush with his and, despite his heavy coat, awareness of his childhood friend struck. Their faces were inches apart with her chin grazing his shoulder. Snow crowned her head and the seriousness in her eyes touched him, eyes that had matured to a mildly exotic tilt above a slender, fragile nose. She was the rare redhead free of freckles. With her prettiness and unaffected candor, Livvy would be the toast of the Marriage Mart, a breath of fresh air for London's open-minded gentlemen—if she was there.

Why was she stuck in this lonely tower?

Small, feminine nostrils flared. "You're staring."

"And you've not let go." His voice was rough and low.

Livvy held on tight, her face turning to Plumtree. The tower's height and elevated Halsey lands gave them a fine view. The church bell tolled the medieval hour Compline, a Christmas Day tradition. Snow dropped a curtain of innocence on jumbled homes where festive candles shined in windows, the effect like polished gold. Ten years he'd been gone. Nothing had changed except a narrow canal cutting through the land. Centuries would pass, but Plumtree would remain the same rustic village.

"I know you're here because of my sneaking into your grandfather's house last night," she said quietly.

She turned, her brown gaze spearing him as if she'd decided to embrace honesty and expected the same of him. His chest squeezed. He swallowed hard. She'd been the one traipsing around dressed as a man, brandishing a pistol at midnight.

Why did *he* feel the heat of expectation?

"Curiosity—perhaps concern?—is getting the best of you. I understand." Her voice was grave. "But, for the moment, we must attend the chair. It's very, very, *very* old. A Roman general or magistrate probably sat on it."

He nodded solemnly. "An ass of great, historical importance."

Livvy bit her bottom lip, fighting a smile. "I am quite serious."

"I see that."

He gave her a sporting smile. This was cozy having a hushed discussion while leaning over a windowsill with Livvy. If he tipped his head toward her, their noses would brush.

Their conversation was a kiss with words.

Her eyes flared wider, and she carried on with an earnest voice. "You must handle this piece with care. All four ivory legs are intact. Do you understand? They are *ivory*." She paused. "This chair is worth a great deal of *money*."

Outside, he hadn't noticed the ivory for the heavy dirt smears, but he did catch how the words ivory and money rolled off her tongue, the syllables full of reverence and need.

"At present, snow is falling on your valuable furniture."

Livvy glanced at snow collecting on the chair. She nodded and, without a word, eased her grip on the rope and backed away from the window. He leaned further out, the advantage of his height, and held the chair away from the wall. Cautiously, he hauled in the rope hand over hand until he set the piece on the floor and untied it.

"Where do you want your prize?"

"If you'd put it there—" she pointed at the east hearth and shut the windows "—I'd be most grateful."

Another canvas cloth was spread across the floor. He placed the relic on the canvas, catching Livvy watching him out of the corner of her eye. A bucket was tucked against the wall, full of paring chisels, a gimlet, pitsaw, and auger among other furniture maker's tools.

Had she stolen tools from the Captain?

Livvy stood at a table, her thumb idly brushing the corner of a mosaic. "The chair is a *curule chair*, unique because it's intact. A discovery from a Roman campsite a farmer uncovered in Learmouth."

"I recall reading about the find. Over a year ago wasn't it?"

"Yes," she said, not meeting his gaze. "The Antiquarian Society was thrilled. To think, it all started when the farmer's plow dug up a Roman sandal."

The Antiquarian Society, or more correctly, *The Antiquarian Society for Historical Study and Preservation,* was an odd lot of historians who loved digging in the earth for pieces of the past. When he was seventeen, Jonas had shoveled dirt, loads of it, on an excavation with Livvy's father in Scotland. The treasure hunt would've been worthwhile, but Mr. Halsey and his antiquarian friends searched the remains of an ancient Pictish village, ecstatic over a broken loom and textile remnants. He smiled, recalling how he and the other laborers had thought the antiquarians a bit daft. Gold was worth a man's excitement; moldy cloth was not.

Hands clamped behind his back, Jonas strolled the circular room. He stepped over a rusted Roman gladius, a soldier's sword, on burlap. Sections of a breast plate rested beside it like pieces of a puzzle to be done. Nothing fit. Mr. Halsey was order itself, yet this room was chaos with artifacts on the floor, a thing the old man would never countenance.

And there was the uncertainty in Livvy's voice.

He stopped at a scribe's desk facing the wall. Scribbled pages cluttered the surface. Four books lined the desk's upper shelf, one name embossed on the spines: Mr. Thomas J. Halsey. Jonas lifted a volume off the shelf.

"Where is your father? Isn't he coming?" He flipped through pages of Viking art styles.

Footsteps scraped behind him. A feminine hand, the nails trimmed short, skin dry at the knuckles reached for the book. Livvy hugged the tome to her brown and yellow stomacher. Torn lace hung from her elbows. Stains streaked her vinegar-scented skirt.

"You know he's not coming."

"I know nothing of the sort."

Her chin lifted. "You haven't figured out what's going on here?"

He drew a patient breath. "Call me dim-witted. Plumtree's fine folk have done as much."

"You are nothing of the sort," she said, her grip relaxing on the book. "You have a quiet strength. Quick to listen and slow to speak, yes. But a dull mind? Never." Her face tilted as if a new facet revealed itself. "You have always been a man of few words. An excellent quality."

The room's glow couldn't match the glimmer in her eyes. He stood taller, basking in Livvy's unexpected praise. Candlelight shined on her mussed copper hair. He wanted to stroke the length of it from the crown of her head to the braid's tip dangling at her tiny waist. The square neck of her bronze-colored gown barely contained plump, white mounds above the book.

"You're not saying much," she murmured, closing the gap between them.

Because the sight of her made his mind spin.

His fingers flexed and curled at his side. The country girl of his youth had grown into a provocative woman with an air of innocence. Coppery wisps traced Livvy's cheek, dangling soft as down on her collarbone. With his gloves still on, he brushed away her loose hair and traced the slanted collarbone to her shoulder and back to the center of her chest. Little goosebumps danced across her breast's upper curve.

Livvy inhaled fast.

"Do you like what I'm saying now?" he asked.

Chapter Three

HIS TOUCH DEMANDED a kiss.

She rocked up on her toes and mashed her lips to his. It was the only way to take control; otherwise Jonas would have the upper hand.

But, he did have the upper hand—smashed to her breast because she'd flung herself at him and his gloved hand had gotten stuck in between. Sensations ricocheted through her body. The aroma of spicy soap, the cool leather on her skin, and five fingers spread wide high on her chest. Nerves singed from his hand resting *there*.

Heat shot to hidden flesh between her legs. She had an older, widowed sister. She knew what was happening.

Unfortunately, nothing *was* happening.

Her mouth locked on his, but neither kissed. What was she supposed to do?

This was nothing like last night's soul-shattering kiss. The element of surprise was hers, and she'd botched it. Horribly.

Dropping back on her heels, she peeked at Jonas. The outer corners of lapis lazuli eyes crinkled above her, taking in the angles of her face before dipping to his gloved hand.

"My hand." Jonas removed it from her breast as one might remove their hold on a fragile dish.

Hugging the Halsey tome, she inched away, unable to look him in the eye. "That was a disaster."

What did she expect? Artful, expert kissing? She spent more time with dusty relics than men. Flirting and kissing were two skills she'd not mastered. Lust was easily understood. What to do with it was another kettle of fish.

"Livvy—"

"Please don't." She swiveled around and returned the book to its shelf. "I don't know what came over me."

"Probably the same thing that overcame me last night."

His rich baritone message soothed her pride, but with every sense jangled, she couldn't face Jonas. Not yet. She gathered papers on her desk and ordered them into two neat stacks and re-ordered them again, willing her cheeks to cool off. They were, no doubt, an unattractive shade of beets.

Snow blew past the tower's lone window. She rubbed her stomacher, the yellow embroidery ripped from catching the jagged ends of broken mosaics.

"I should be a gentleman and leave," he said to her back.

"But you're not going to, are you?"

"No."

She swung around and rested both hands on the desk behind her. "You have a talent for leaving when I want you to stay, and staying when I'd prefer you go."

Jonas pulled a chair out from the work table. He turned it backward and straddled the seat. During her desk organizing, he'd removed his hat, gloves, and heavy outer coat. Blue velvet stretched across wide shoulders, the coat flapping open with a casual air. Black leather breeches molded to his thighs, the cut showing he'd patronized one of London's finer tailors. Pirating must have been lucrative, indeed. The Jonas of her youth wore ill-fitting homespun and when he grew larger, the Captain's oft-mended cast-offs.

With Jonas's good looks and natty attire, most women would see a dashing man. She saw Plumtree's quiet rebel son, the young man who'd claimed he didn't care about wearing patched-up clothes.

Her heart softened. She knew better.

"You look rather comfortable," she said. "Planning to stay awhile?"

"Long enough for you to explain yourself." His gaze roved over broken pottery. "What are you're doing in here?"

Jonas was leaving England for good. She *could* tell him. Confession was good for the soul. Who better to unburden herself with than a childhood friend? A confidence shared with Jonas would be a confidence kept.

But, this was a Christmas Day visit, a time when most souls hunkered down with family.

"I could ask the same of you. Why are you here and not with your grandfather?"

Jaw resting in the flat of his hand, his smile was tolerant. "If my worst sin is a short walk in the country, consider me guilty. You, on the other hand, have your share of secrets. Time to 'fess up."

Secrets and sins. They could be one and the same where she was concerned. She couldn't toss out a quip or clamber out a window to escape this. Her reckoning was coming.

To begin it with Jonas could be freeing.

She pulled a thin volume off the desk shelf and passed it to Jonas. "My big secret is this."

He read aloud the gold-embossed spine. *"An Exhaustive Study of Vallum Hadriani* by Thomas J. Halsey."

"I wrote it." She waited, her brows pinching. Relief didn't come.

"You wrote the book in your father's name?"

"After he took ill last year. His notes, my words. I was at his side when he wrote most of them...have been since you left." Her chin tipped high. "I may not have a university education, but I know as much as any antiquarian. I've been on nearly all my father's summer excavations, helping him catalogue Roman relics."

Jonas skimmed the volume in hand. His keen study wandered from the page to the table's historic treasures before drifting back to the desk with its neat stacks of paper.

"You're writing another one in his name," his deep voice intoned.

"Yes."

His face grave, Jonas set the book on the work table and folded his arms on the chair's back rest. The toe of her shoe traced circles on the floor as if she were a girl caught cheating on her sums. This was supposed to be freeing, this confession to a friend, but the grim line of Jonas's mouth made her push off the desk and pace the floor.

"Say something, please." She wiped damp palms down her skirts. "I can't bear this silence."

"Livvy, surely you don't plan to continue this deception. The Antiquarian Society will eventually find out." He nodded at the desk. "Your father's publisher will, too, I suspect."

"I know." Heels striking the floor, her voice dripped with misery. "I didn't intend for everything to go this far."

"One thing I learned while in service to the Earl of Greenwich, academic societies set great store on the integrity of their field of study."

She walked the wide planks, wringing her hands. "It was only supposed to be that volume behind you."

"What happened?"

She sighed heavily, looking to the pristine world beyond the window. "Fame from the Learmouth find." Her pacing took her to the mullioned glass. "The book I wrote in my father's name did well...better than his others."

"Cause for celebration."

"In a way, it was. I've always wanted to write fiction. Adventures about Roman generals." She touched the window with both hands, a woman trapped in a world of her own making. "And then Father's publisher sent a letter last month requesting a book on the Learmouth excavation."

"And you said yes."

"The offer was too good to turn down. Of course, they don't want me. They want Thomas J. Halsey."

"And you're taking up your father's work until his return."

The frosted glass chilled her palms. A long-held ache rolled from her belly into her chest, lodging itself behind her breastbone.

"He'll never work again, Jonas. He's dying." Her forlorn voice drifted through the tower. Lonely. Sad. A little lost. Her father was the sun and the moon to her.

Chair legs scraped behind her. Steady footfalls crossed the floor. Looking up, the stalwart face of her friend reflected in the glass behind her. Silent. Comforting. A man easy to be with.

The same man she'd kissed hotly one night and with disastrous results moments ago.

Jonas didn't ask for her father's tale. Nor did he hug her as he'd done the day she'd told him her beloved cat, Julius Caesar, had died. She was eleven years old, then. Tears had flowed that day and big-hearted Jonas had wrapped his arms around her until she could cry no more.

Was he trying to keep his distance now?

He might want safe detachment. She did not. The tale was already started. She'd see it finished.

"Summer of last year, we were at the Learmouth excavation. Everything was going well, except Father complained of his arm tingling. He insisted on climbing a tree to get a birds-eye view of the site," she said, staring at the peaceful world beyond the tower. "When he was in the tree, a spasm wracked his body and he fell."

"But he survived."

"He did, but he hasn't been the same since...in body or mind."

"The Captain thinks your father works with you here in the tower."

Warming both hands on her skirt, she faced Jonas. "Because Mother and I need everyone to believe it. At least until this book is published and—" she tipped her head to the hearth "—that chair sells. We know we can't keep up this ruse for much longer."

"Your father is infirm?"

"Infirm?" A pitiful laugh rippled through her. "This summer, he walked with a cane. Now he's bedridden."

"With no chance for recovery?"

"None." Her eyes squeezed shut and she hugged herself, needing blessed blankness. "Most days, he doesn't recognize me...his own daughter."

"An ailment of the mind," Jonas said softly. "And you are carrying the weight of providing for your family."

"I do what I can." Head resting on the wall, she opened her eyes. "It's why I broke into your bedchamber. I stole his old watch from you."

"The watch I won in a card game?"

"Yes." Her voice thinned. "It's baffling. He doesn't recognize me, but Father can recall certain personal objects with perfect clarity. He kept badgering Mother about his watch, fixating on it. He didn't know it was gone. The physician said it's good to surround Father with things he does remember. Helps his mind. So, when I heard you were in Plumtree…"

"You decided to get it back."

"I didn't think you'd miss it."

"If it brings him comfort, keep it." He chuckled and set his hands on his hips. "You know you could've asked me for it. I'd have given it to you."

"And risk having to explain why?" She shook her head. "I couldn't take that chance."

Jonas smarted as if she'd flung ale in his face. Hands still on his hips, he shook his head, taking great interest in the toes of his boots. She took a half-step off the wall and stopped when blue eyes pinned her.

"Livvy, you know you can trust me, same as ever."

But I can't count on you to stay.

"Thank you, Jonas." She gave him a thin-lipped, obligatory smile. "Please understand, I couldn't be sure…"

"Because I've given you no reason to be sure."

"There is that. You are leaving."

"Yes. There is that," he said, his voice sad and final.

Tucking hair behind her ear, she tried for a cheerier smile. "I am grateful for your help bringing up the chair, but I must get back to work."

Daylight faded outside. She donned her shawl and walked stiff-limbed to the hearth. Crouching low, she touched a taper to an ember.

Behind her, she expected Jonas to gather his things and leave the tower. She was graceless when it came to social niceties. Elspeth would know what to do. Her sister always did. But, really, was there a pleasant way to do this? Dismiss a long-lost friend?

Jonas bored holes in her as she lit candles set at intervals on the work tables. Globs of dried wax mucking up the table attested to long nights in the tower. At her desk, she lit an iron candle stand. Her side vision caught Jonas kneeling in front of the curule chair.

"Are you restoring all these artifacts?" he asked.

"The smaller pieces, yes." She blew out the taper. "It's the larger items like that chair that bedevil me."

"I can fix this." He bent lower, inspecting the joint where ivory attached to wood. "Since I'm not leaving until Twelfth Night ends, I may as well do some good. It'll give me something to do."

"Won't the Captain miss you?"

"He'll miss the chance to harangue me about taking over the family business." Jonas tested fragile hinges on the chair. An eye to the rusted metal, he shrugged off his coat. "Take this, will you?"

She held the blue velvet, a mute witness to Jonas bending this way and that. A touch to another hinge. A thoughtful hum as his fingertips ran the length of all four chair legs. Capable hands testing, poking, skimming ancient wood with the gentleness a surgeon gave a desperate patient. Last night, her senses sung a different tune when studying those hands.

"Finding anything I should know about?" she asked.

He slanted a grin at her. "Yes. This old wood is telling me I should work on it."

"*You?* Pardon me, Jonas," she said to his profile. "But you don't know one jot or tittle about Roman antiquities. Your offer is generous, but I'm not sure it's wise."

He chuckled, examining the upper arch. "Your Roman chair, it's furniture. Don't forget, I come from generations of furniture makers."

"Which you turned your back on ten years ago. This isn't a practice piece."

His hands grazed the back rest's upper curve, pausing to push a spot as if he tested a wound. "I'm aware of the gravity here. You forget. The Captain apprenticed me when I was eleven years old."

Hugging his velvet coat, she couldn't argue with his experience. While she spent time with tutors, Jonas had learned the cabinetmaker's trade at his grandfather's side. He tilted the chair into the hearth's light, his forefinger tracing knobby carvings. Jonas checked wood flecks on his finger. He even sniffed the wood.

"Some rot here, but the rest of this arch is intact. If you won't let me work on it, you'd better have a care how deep you work the grain or you'll split it in two."

"You see that in the grain?"

"I do." He stood up and dusted off his hands.

She passed back his coat. "You really think you can save it? Even the hinges? After the ivory legs, those hinges and the carvings will be what collectors inspect the most."

Jonas slid into his blue velvet coat. "You're selling this to collectors?"

"One collector. He has a number of interested buyers, if the chair remains intact."

"I'll need to borrow some of the Captain's tools, but that shouldn't be a problem," he said, collecting his heavy coat and hat and gloves.

She folded the ends of her shawl over her chest amused at her refusal of Jonas's help turning into a discussion of *how* he would help. "Your working on this chair would free me to write the next book."

"In your father's name? Or yours?"

"My father's. No one will accept my name on a manuscript."

"Why not? You were spouting facts about Londinium and Roman generals when you were ten years old."

Her nose wrinkled. "Irritating, wasn't it?"

"Endearing."

His lone word, said in his deep rumble of a voice, satisfied her to her toes. Fragile threads of friendship strengthened on his singular affirmation. The truth was Jonas understood her. He always had.

"I'm afraid it will be my hand on the manuscript and Thomas J. Halsey on the book." She fixed her shawl again, pulling the wool tighter. "Once the book is done and the curule chair restored, I plan to put this all behind me."

Jonas rubbed gold trim on his tricorne, a gentlemanly smile ghosting his mouth. "We'll have a few weeks. We can manage it together."

Firelight shined on his tall, black boots. Jonas was handsome but not in the conventional sense. He was big, his size akin to braw Highlanders. Town gentlemen were tame by comparison. Jonas would never spout flowery phrases or write poetic letters. But, he'd keep a secret and be the friend to catch you if you fell from an adventure that went awry.

And her heart ached that he'd not be around to catch her again.

This was all she'd have. A few weeks with Jonas.

The hat rotated in his hands, a sluggish end-over-end circle as his gaze locked with hers. "Well, I expect the Captain and his cronies are impatiently awaiting my return."

"Yes," she said, her voice quiet. "You should get back to your grandfather and his guests."

Jonas stepped around the Roman chair, his broad shoulders seeming to take up the room. She followed his blue velvet-covered back as he picked his way through the relic-strewn floor to the stairs. He slipped on his black frock coat and black tricorne in silence. Her palm pressed her stomacher. Butterflies camped there.

"You will be back tomorrow?" she called out. "To fix the chair."

Jonas gave her a swoon-worthy smile. "Bright and early."

She'd never swooned a day in her life, but her knees didn't know that. They were jelly. "Bright and early. I look forward to it."

He disappeared down the winding stairs. She froze in place, listening to his descending steps until the old oak door scraped open and shut. Grabbing her skirts, she sprinted to the window to watch Jonas walk home. Winter covered the evening world in white. Bits of diamonds could be scattered in the snow, sparkling beautifully. Jonas emerged from the side of the tower, trudging through the fluff. Light from her window cast a mellow glow on the ground, and Jonas walked through it. Gentle wind trifled with his coat. His black boots stopped their trudge. He turned and waved. Nose pressed to cold glass, she waved back.

Was it possible his blue eyes shined clearer and more lively? *For her?* Palm flat on the icy window, she felt Jonas, his warmth and presence lingering until he disappeared in the night.

Chapter Four

"IT DOES MY heart good to see those tools in your hand again." The Captain picked up a small chisel, the sharp tip no bigger than a child's littlest finger. "You'll want this, too, though it needs sharpening."

The barn-cum-workshop of Braithwaite Furniture and Sons hinted at days past. Patterns for Chippendale chair backs hung from hooks high on a wall from the grandest to humblest designs. Dusty cobwebs fluttered in the corners. Jonas quietly rolled up the chisels and tucked them in his leather satchel. Silence was best when the Captain waxed on about him taking over the business—a thing both men knew would never happen.

The Captain's eyes narrowed to shrewd slits. "A young man strong as you can do twice the work I did. Oversee twice the laborers…make a tidy income."

A young man as strong as he was? No. He'd shake Plumtree's dust off his feet the same as he did ten years ago and leave behind the ridicule.

Big Ox. Dumb oaf. Brainless beast of a man.

Villagers had admonished him in his youth, *"Better to use your God-given brawn to make your way in the world, because the good Lord gave your brother all the brains."*

The sting of old taunts haunted him the moment he'd stepped foot in Plumtree two nights ago. He tried to shake them, but the past wouldn't let go.

Jonas picked up a planer off the workbench, words of the past blistering his soul as if freshly spoke. The Captain had held this same tool, saying years ago, *"Your brother will attend St. Mary's College and study the law. You—" The Captain smoothed the planer up and down the walnut board, wood shavings dropping around his feet. "—you're better suited to a life of labor. Right here. This shop shall be yours."*

Even the Captain, good man that he was, had unwittingly elevated Jacob over Jonas. His mother had patted Jonas's arm and bade him to consider the merits of furniture-making. *Take over the Braithwaite Furniture and Sons*, the Captain and his mother had said.

Instead, Jonas had set fire to the building.

It was an accident, a small fire, as damaging blazes go. Jonas had placed linseed oil too close to an open flame and *whoosh!* One beam had been charred to ruin and a fine oak chest of drawers for meant for an earl's butler had been reduced to ash. The fire had branded him an ungrateful youth in the eyes of Plumtree. Once the destruction was repaired, Jonas packed his things and left as quietly as he'd arrived at the tender age of ten.

The Captain slapped the work bench, snapping Jonas out of the past. "In its finer days, a man could expect three hundred fifty pounds income."

His grandfather ambled the rough-hewn floors, speaking around his pipe, his cane tapping the floor. The old man wasn't giving up. Jonas gathered twine, listening as patiently as a grandson ready to leave could.

"Did I tell you Chippendale's man of business inquired about Braithwaite Furniture and Sons constructing a series of lady's writing desks?"

Jonas tossed two balls of twine in his satchel. "Odd, since you haven't been open for business of late."

The Captain chewed his pipe. "Oh, very well. I wrote Chippendale first. Told him my grandson was coming home." And his grandfather was off, his enthusiasm churning. "Just think of it. My experience and your strong back."

"You mean a beast of a man like me...a man with no brains." He picked up a rusted hammer and dropped it back in the bucket.

His grandfather winced. "You can't still believe that."

Jonas tied the satchel. "I don't." *But the sting of those words will take a long time to fade.*

The Captain gripped his cane with both hands, his proud shoulders bowing with age. Or was it grandfatherly guilt at not stemming the critical tide that had washed over Jonas years ago? The old man had always walked through life with his brand of salty-tongued dignity.

His thin lids drooped. "You found your own way. Seeing the world, returning to England and taking a position as man of business for the Earl of Greenwich. That was no small feat. Everyone in the village was quite impressed."

"And there's more world I want to see," Jonas said, tossing the leather satchel over his shoulder. He was long past caring about Plumtree's good opinion of him.

"By the time I was your age, I'd been married, fathered three children, and buried two of them. Surely you'll want a wife."

"And settle into Braithwaite cottage?" He scoffed. "Plumtree's too small for my taste."

"It welcomed you and your brother," the Captain said sharply.

"And shamed my mother."

"She eventually won them over," was the best the old man could give.

Jonas eyed his grandfather under the brim of his hat. "A thing she should *never* have had to do."

The village's cool, dismissive matrons had cut the deepest. Women were cruelest to other women. His mother bore the shunning with a stiff spine, but sometimes he'd find her teary-eyed in a quiet corner at home. His boyish arms around her was the only cure he could give.

The family had borne the brunt of ridicule until the town's folk moved on to better gossip. Eventually, the hardest hearts melted under Jacob's charm, a thing Jonas didn't possess. He was the twin to stand stoically aside while his brother won Plumtree's hearts with wit and undeniable friendliness. It came in handy when they got into scrapes such as freeing Farmer Watson's prize-winning pig…and then chasing the sow through the village, sliding through muddy roads, their antics splashing mud on pedestrians.

Later, Braithwaite handsomeness served a purpose. Tavern wenches and merchant's daughters threw themselves at Jacob and Jonas. Conversation wasn't required when a pretty girl did all the talking. None truly noticed the *person* Jonas was. None, that is, except for lank-limbed Livvy Halsey, as ready for a day of fishing as she was to climb trees and catch frogs.

Her pert smile and saucy tongue had been a sylph-like memory all these years since he'd left, a comfort in lonely days at sea. Those were the times a man saw the deepest nooks and crannies of his soul. One face appeared often when he stared at wide open water.

Livvy Halsey.

When it came to pretty Elspeth, he couldn't recall her features with nearly the same vividness as Livvy's—Plumtree's best and brightest spot.

Funny that.

"Plumtree has changed since you left. At least consider the merits of reacquainting yourself with the district," the Captain said, a slow smile creasing his face. "Give the fair young women here a chance. There are many festivities planned from now until Twelfth Night."

Jonas's hand curled tighter on the satchel. "I'm not long for Plumtree, sir." He tipped his head at the Captain. "Now, if you'll excuse me, I promised to assist the Halseys in repairing a chair."

They strolled to the workshop's open door with Jonas slowing his step in deference to his grandfather. They walked together into morning sunshine, and Jonas shut the door after them.

"For all your protests of leaving Plumtree, you haven't said what you want me to do with your inheritance," the Captain said to Jonas's back. "This land, the cottage, the shop…it will be yours."

Jonas latched a rusted lock on the door. "What about Jacob? Doesn't he want it?"

"He's a solicitor, not a furniture maker. Working with wood is not in his blood."

"And you think it's in mine?"

The Captain leaned both hands on his cane, his blue eyes twinkling on the satchel bulging with tools. "Something's got your blood stirring."

Jonas ignored the quip and dug the shop's key from his pocket. "Here."

"Keep it. You may need more tools in this endeavor of yours with the Halseys." The Captain struck out for the cottage.

Jonas dropped the iron key back in his pocket. "Please let Mrs. Addington know I'll be on time for dinner."

The Captain paused, his snowy white beard showing as he angled his face to the Halsey Tower. "I will."

The old man trekked on, his footfalls and the cane a quiet plod on snow and gravel. Jonas's heart squeezed at his grandfather's aged amble. Once powerful shoulders stooped. The old man had borne the weight of family, providing for him and his brother and mother. Never once did his grandfather say a recriminating word to his daughter for bearing sons out of wedlock. If he did, Jonas had never heard it.

The proud head, once thick with Braithwaite black hair, was pure white, tied in a small queue brushing his coat collar.

The Captain had given his all for his family.

And none would be here to comfort him in his final years.

Jonas waited for the Captain to get safely inside before making his way to the orchard. Sun poured down on Plumtree. He squinted at a blinding white world of snow, save the bare, tangled branches of the Braithwaite orchard. Sunlight glittered on the diamond panes of Halsey Tower's window. Was Livvy already there?

She was a balm to his soul. Sweet yet saucy. Even her sudden kiss yesterday blended the best parts of her, soft lips, curious and knowing at the same time. He should've wrapped his arms around her and kissed her back, but she was off him in a trice, embarrassed. He'd wanted to let her recover and try again, but Livvy fidgeted against her desk, pouring out bigger and more important things like family secrets.

Kissing would have to wait.

He trudged up the meadow to her tower, his mouth pulling a grim line. Who had taught Livvy how to kiss? One of Farmer Watson's sons? A laborer on her father's excavations? Or another antiquarian? Probably a man university educated and smart. His boots sunk in a deep pocket of snow.

Or the appropriate Will Hastings with his Eton education and impeccable manners?

Cresting the Halsey knoll, he bristled at the sight of six chimneys in the east puffing thin streams of smoke. Hastings Manor, a grand home belonging to a grand family. No Braithwaite darkened their door except to deliver a repaired table at the servant's entrance.

Childhood flattened Plumtree's social field until he and all the village boys sprouted chin hairs. That's when the stark social divide came. The Halsey girls were the bridge.

Up ahead, the familiar rope hung from the tower. The end of it was tied to a modest-sized crate in the snow. Voices drifted from the tower's open window. Jonas strolled around the tower and pushed the door left ajar. On quiet feet, he made his way up the winding stairs, the voices getting louder.

"I can't countenance you spending an entire day alone with Jonas Braithwaite."

Jonas halted his progress. *Mrs. Halsey?* Her continental accent spun elegantly around each word she said.

"But you *can* countenance the eight hundred pounds we'll get if he repairs the curule chair." Livvy. Her voice pitched headstrong as ever.

"Do not be impertinent."

"I am being practical, Mother. Jonas has kindly agreed to restore the chair *and* keep quiet about father's condition."

Mrs. Halsey sighed. "You should never have let him into the tower."

"What was I supposed to do? It was Christmas Day. I didn't expect anyone to come calling and he saved me from scraping the chair up the outer wall."

"It's simply not proper. Your father let you have your headstrong ways far too long. He thought it enchanting," Mrs. Halsey said, her voice a tad weary. "I should've hired a governess straightaway and not waited as I did."

"Elspeth and I turned out fine."

"You could do with a better sense of decorum."

"Decorum is highly overrated." Livvy's voice gentled with affection. "You and Father gave me the best childhood a girl could want."

Silence stretched for a heartbeat. There was a sniffle. A murmur of sound.

"And now we lean heavily on you, my girl," Mrs. Halsey said sadly. "Too much, I fear."

Shoes scraped the floor as if mother and daughter embraced. Jonas balked at eavesdropping on an intimate moment. The upper floor's light flooded the top of the stairs. Below him, the tower's door remained ajar. He tarried in the dark space in between, an interloper. He could escape. Or he could go forward and announce his presence.

One hand on the cold stone wall, he swallowed a hard truth. He was good at hanging in the periphery. Not quite present for those in need. Quick to hold his feelings in check and quick to leave when a storm of emotions kicked up. He'd never mastered the fine art of understanding the outer reaches of feelings. Perhaps that's why he and Lord Edward, Earl of Greenwich, got on so famously. Neither truly understood women or emotions well.

But, even the reclusive Earl of Greenwich had found love.

Jonas's fingertips dug into the ancient stone wall. Would he ever find love?

"You don't need to worry about improprieties, Mother. Everyone thinks Father and I are working here. Jonas visiting the tower will have no social consequence." Livvy sniffled, her voice a touch amused. "He still regards me as the bothersome girl in braids."

"You can't know that," her mother chided.

A knowing laugh echoed above his head. "Yes, I can. I kissed him yesterday and he didn't kiss me back. It was awkward."

"Olivia," her mother groaned.

"You could have another governess watch over me," Livvy teased. "But it's a bit late at my ripe age of twenty-four."

"You are not a child, my dear, I know this."

"Then you will trust me working with Jonas."

"I'd feel better if you called him Mr. Braithwaite." A tolerant, motherly sigh drifted through the tower. "At least Mr. Haggerty will be here soon. He promises to come once the roads are clear enough for travel."

Standing in the shadows, a pang of conscience pinched Jonas for eavesdropping. He pushed loudly up the stairs, his boots heavy on each step as he called out, "Good morning to the tower."

He breached the upper floor's light to the startled Halsey women. Mrs. Halsey stood as tall as Livvy, her brown eyes flaring wide, the mildly exotic tilt of her eyes a gift from mother to daughter. Lines etched their outer corners, and a faint pallor marked her features. Dressed in deep purple, her graying auburn hair swept high off her forehead. She was rustic elegance, though not of English stock. Rumor had it she hailed from the Commonwealth of Lithuania, the daughter of an antiquarian.

Livvy smiled at him, her thick copper-colored braid curving over her shoulder, the tip dangling where black lacing nipped her waist. A very pleasant, very male bolt shot through him, beginning at his heart and landing in the placket of his breeches.

"Good morning, Jonas. You are looking hale and hearty," Mrs. Halsey said, one brow arching. "And with a gold earring no less."

He removed his tricorne and sketched a bow. "A necessary evil when I took to the seas."

"Then, you weren't a pirate." She smiled, folding both hands before her.

He flashed a chaste grin at Livvy and removed his coat. "No, ma'am."

"The people of Plumtree entertained themselves with tales of your plunders on the high seas. At least until the Captain disabused them."

Head canting to one side, she studied him. "This renown matters not to you, I think."

"It does not, ma'am."

Livvy tucked both hands behind her back, smiling boldly at him. "I think Mr. Braithwaite looks like a gentleman of fortune."

Her voice did things to him, made him want to listen to her for the pure joy of hearing her voice. How had he missed that yesterday? Livvy Halsey trod a different path than London's frothy misses. Would any of those well-bred young women don breeches and climb trees to give their father a token of comfort in his last days? Livvy Halsey was all heart, a woman who wore her keen mind and adventurous spirit well.

Clamping both hands behind his back, he stood ramrod straight. "I was third mate on the *Carlotta* for Sanford Shipping Company. Simple as that. I'm sure you've heard of the *Carlotta*? It was the Earl of Greenwich's ship for his naturalist voyage."

"Indeed." Mrs. Halsey eyed the gold earring. "I've read his pamphlets on the healing properties of African plants."

Her refined manners wouldn't allow probing questions about the gold on his ear. He decided to save her the trouble of stewing over the odd gold piece.

"If you're wondering about the earring...the lot of us had our ears pierced at a port in the West Indies." He grinned, his chin dipping a fraction. "You could say there was much whiskey involved...that and the fear of God that should our bodies wash ashore from a shipwreck, the gold would pay for a proper Christian burial."

Mrs. Halsey smiled back. "The same reasoning pirates give."

"Very true, ma'am. Your knowledge of the seas shouldn't surprise me given your experience with other topics."

"I was a young woman once," she said archly. "The appeal of a dashing man is not lost on me."

"Age has no bearing with you, ma'am. Little slips past your notice."

Mrs. Halsey's laughter tinkled like a bell. "Jonas Braithwaite, you have come into your own. What a fine gentleman you are." She looked askance between Livvy and Jonas, her tone knowing. "It is a good thing you are not long for Plumtree, or I would have to play chaperone."

"Your daughter's honor is safe with me."

A kind glow lit her eyes. "As I believe it always has been."

"I am standing beside you, Mother," Livvy piped up.

Mrs. Halsey kissed her daughter's cheek. "I know, dear, but I will always be your mother." Looking to Jonas, she gave a regal nod to the curule chair sitting on a table. "Do you think you can bring life into the chair? Olivia says she informed you of its tremendous historic value." She paused as if choosing her words with care. "You understand. We need a good...*outcome* in the sale of this artifact."

He patted the satchel he'd dropped beside his coat and strode the long way around the table. "Yes, ma'am. I am up to the challenge—" He set the leather bag down "—and I am aware of the chair's importance."

Livvy met him at the table and opened book set near the chair. "I found these diagrams of other curule chairs. I thought they'd help."

Her ink-stained fingers smoothed a faded forest green gown, this one free of lacey elbows.

"Olivia tells me you graciously returned Mr. Halsey's old watch," Mrs. Halsey said, her eyes glossy and bright. "For that, I am most grateful."

"I'm pleased to bring some comfort to your family." Jonas felt his ears warm from the admiration in her eyes. He swallowed the knot in his throat and untied the satchel. The Halsey family had always been kind to him. "I shall get to work, then."

"I brought food." She motioned to a basket covered with a red and white checked cloth. "Should you need anything else, please come to the house. Otherwise, I'll take my leave and let the two of you get to work."

"Thank you, ma'am." Jonas unrolled the cloth full of chisels and set them on the table in order from smallest to largest.

Livvy wrapped her black shawl around her shoulders and took her place at the desk. She pulled a pen knife from her desk and shaved the tip of a new quill, the scrape a gentle noise in the tower. The hearth's fire crackled and Mrs. Halsey's heel strikes sounded on the floors. Jonas picked up the smallest chisel, his thumb testing its sharpness.

Quaint stillness settled around him. Touching the tools was another step into the better parts of his past. Though Jonas loathed admitting it, he liked working with his hands. The wood, the tools satisfied him.

Mrs. Halsey's tinkling laughter rose to the rafters. "I truly have nothing to worry about here, do I?"

Livvy swiveled in her chair. "Mother, *please.*"

"Do not forget the crate outside." She smiled benignly. "If the two of you make good progress, you should reward yourselves with a night of fun."

Jonas set down the chisel and walked to the window. He'd forgotten about the crate.

"What fun?" At the window, warmth and sunshine blasted him, the feel of it good on his skin as he grabbed the rope. Or was it being in the tower with Livvy?

"The festivities will be hosted at the Sheep's Head tonight. Are you and the Captain planning to attend?"

"The Captain mentioned an invitation but I hadn't thought about it," he said, hauling up the crate.

"It's a costume party, Mother. I don't have anything to wear."

"Nor do I." He hefted the light crate through the window.

Mrs. Halsey tapped her steepled fingers. "The two of you are cleverer. You could come up with something."

Jonas set the straw-filled crate on the floor. "I'm of a mind to spend a quiet night at home."

"Nonsense," the older woman retorted. "You are both young. You would do me a great favor, Mr. Braithwaite, if you made certain my daughter has a night of frivolity. She has labored too long in here...she'll turn into one of these relics if she's not careful."

Livvy groaned and turned back to her desk.

Jonas dusted off both hands. "I'll see what I can do to convince her, ma'am."

"Very good." Mrs. Halsey smiled and slipped out of sight, her footsteps echoing her departure.

Livvy kicked off one shoe and tucked her foot under her bottom. She dipped a nib on the ink and began writing. Her other foot swung back and forth as if keeping time with her flow of words. Finding his way to the chair, Jonas was once again tongue-tied. The idea of a night with Livvy settled on him. He knew Livvy the girl, but Olivia Halsey, the woman? He couldn't say.

Did she want him to know her? There was the matter of their kisses. The first night, hot and salacious. The second afternoon, tentative and flat.

He wanted another try.

Standing at the table, he set out the rest of his tools. Work was an elixir. It gave him purpose and pride. To be the one to help save the Halseys from imminent disaster satisfied him. A night of fun with Livvy would too.

They worked in silence, the time measured by Livvy's quiet scratches on paper. An hour or two or three passed with the hearth's fire at this back. He etched his chisel through one decorative carving after another on the chair's top arch. Slivers of wood dropped onto the table around the ivory legs. He stepped back and ran a finger across fresh wood, contentment swelling in his chest.

"There's something satisfactory in saving a piece of history." Livvy's voice broke the silence.

He glanced over his shoulder. Livvy set one hand at her back and stretched like a cat, the shawl falling off her shoulders. Black lacing cinched her tiny waist between lush upper and lower curves. How easily he could untie it...set her hourglass shape free. He'd rub the small of her back with attentive circles, make her feel better, and then he'd let his carnal nature take command.

"Jonas?" Her head cocked.

He snapped out of his lustful haze and massaged his nape. "Getting hungry."

Livvy slipped from her chair and padded over to the basket. She set out a feast of bread, dried apples, cheese, and ham all while chattering about her progress with the manuscript and his progress with the chair. He stared hungrily at her. Yes, there was something satisfactory in uncovering the chair's beauty. Staring at Livvy's plump lips and soft-skinned face, there was deeper satisfaction in discovering a woman's beauty. Livvy Halsey was a beauty by any man's standards.

Had he been too busy being her friend to give adequate tribute to her?

Or was Livvy content to stay in the safe parameters of friendship after their disastrous kiss?

Tonight's festivities at the Sheep's Head would be the perfect foil to laugh again and have fun. He'd convince her to attend the village entertainment and, when the time was right, he'd test the bounds of friendship.

Chapter Five

"**H**E'S RATHER LIKE my favorite hunting hound. Nose at attention, ready for action. Question is *who* does he wait for?" Mr. Goodspeak doled out this insight while sizing up the Sheep Head's newest dartboard.

"Hard to say with the black mask on." Mr. Littlewood peered at Jonas from the pine wood settle tucked into their section of the Sheep's Head.

Jonas leaned a casual shoulder against the wall, the Sheep's Head door in his sight line. A slender tavern maid dressed like a shepherdess plunked four cups brimming with mulled wine on the table. Jonas fished out the necessary shillings and dropped them into her outstretched hand. She brushed a panniered hip against his thighs, eyeing him over her shoulder as she sashayed to the bar rife with pine boughs.

Mr. Meakin held his cup to his bottom lip. "Methinks our boy just got an invitation from the shepherdess."

Mr. Goodspeak hummed thoughtfully, one eye squinting at the dartboard. "My money's not on the shepherdess." He lobbed the dart and missed the board entirely.

"With luck like that you won't have money to wager a'tall my good man," Mr. Meakin said, chortling in his cup.

Mr. Littlefield removed a clove floating in his wine. "Whoever it is, she hasn't arrived yet."

"You realize, gentlemen, I am right here," Jonas said in good humor.

Mr. Meakin's knees cracked as he rose from his chair to take his turn at the dartboard. "Just a spot of fun m'boy, enjoying what we can of Plumtree's den of iniquity."

Jonas took a long swallow of his wine, the spicy cinnamon and clove flavors rich in his throat. He'd held this spot for the better part of an hour. The Sheep's Head was a far cry from a den of iniquity, but Plumtree's normally staid residents were out in full force, pushing the bounds of decorum. One man pinched a serving maid's bottom. She yelped and gave him a tongue lashing. Another woman lolled on the lap of a strapping man dressed as a plague doctor. Throngs milled the smoky room, laughter bouncing off timbered rafters. Men and women alike slurped pints of ale and mulled wine. Half the comers wore elaborate costumes from the new blacksmith dressed as a medieval Welsh archer to his friend boasting a Henry the Eighth doublet. The rest of the revelers brushed off their garb and wore their best smiles.

The Captain was conspicuously absent, claiming an ailing head. Jonas was glad his grandfather wasn't here. The Captain's shrewd eyes would see Jonas dancing attendance on Livvy Halsey, and the old man would sing the praises of Plumtree's finest maid. He slid two fingers inside his cravat as if the marital noose had settled around his throat.

He *would* leave Plumtree. But a night of fun with Livvy—

The door opened and four bodies stumbled in, their heads tipped with frivolity. He locked onto one familiar face masked in black lace. The woman's eyes scanned the public house. He waited. His body tensed. He could hear himself breathe while he waited for her to see him. Livvy searched the room, her fingers unhooking her cloak's frogs under her chin until her stare touched his.

His belly clenched. Her hands stilled. The moment was perfect, taut with expectation. A promise of what *could* happen hung between them. Livvy felt it. Her plump, flesh pink lips parted, and he'd swear he could see the diminutive dark space between them—a small soft part, begging to be kissed.

For his kiss.

The power of it.

The desire. It cast a lure between them.

The rush inside his body breathed new life into him. There'd be no bad kisses tonight. With Livvy, even thoughts of their awkward kiss made him smile. Only a woman like her could make a man think that.

He pushed off the wall. This potent connection with Livvy sent a slow burn through his chest. Carnal sensations landed in the skin between his legs…teased his balls…played havoc with flesh tucked deep in his placket. The twinge was as pleasant as it was painful.

Holding Livvy's attention across the room, he told the Captain's friends, "Don't bother to wait for me tonight, gentlemen."

Did the men mumble at his back? Jonas couldn't say. He advanced on the newcomers, his focus locked on the copper-haired woman staring at him. A laughing woman in a gold mask pulled Livvy's cloak from her shoulders, and his step faltered.

Livvy wore homespun breeches, a gentleman's bottle green coat, and familiar scrubby, black boots.

Was she sending him a saucy message with her choice of costume?

A smile split his face. Above the sea of revelers, he gave her a knowing nod and descended on the newest arrivals. The corners of Livvy's mouth curled with a cat-like smile. A game was afoot, one as old as time. Friendship and flirtation would blur tonight.

Her chin tipped a degree. She breathed deeply thrusting out her breasts, showing part of her costume was not the same. A black waistcoat covered Livvy's spectacular bosom. He was sure a proper corset did too under each mannish layer of clothes. A hearty clap on his shoulder shook him out of his Livvy-induced trance.

"Jonas Braithwaite, I'd heard you'd come home." Will Hastings plucked off his gloves in rapid order. "It is good to see you, old boy."

"Hastings." Jonas gave a quick bow. "Good to see you."

"It has been a long time."

"Ten years."

"Truly? That long?" Will fisted a glove-filled hand on his hip, his eyes clouding as if he counted the years. "Hmmm…I suppose it has. You'll remember my sister, Miss Emma Hastings. Last you saw her, she was playing with dolls under the watchful eye of her nurse."

Miss Hastings rolled her eyes and sketched a curtsey.

"Allow me to introduce you to her friend, Lady Rowena Gage." Hastings pivoted to Livvy. "Of course you remember Miss Olivia Halsey...all grown up now."

"I remember," he said, stiffening. He'd forgotten that no one must know about his visits to her tower.

"Mr. Braithwaite. It's good to see you again, all hale and hearty, sir." Livvy's voice was a smoky promise.

"Hale and hearty, indeed. Big Ox. Isn't that what I called you when we were boys swimming the River Trent?"

Jonas smiled, gritting his teeth. No doubt Will thought Big Ox a fun boyhood name. "I can't recall."

Livvy frowned at Mr. Hastings but the jocular man was too busy stuffing his gloves in his coat pocket to notice. Did she find the childhood sobriquet distasteful? Her eyes expanded within her mask as if chiding Jonas, *Tell him not to call you that!*

His answer was the smallest of shrugs.

"We can reminisce over a pint. Will you join us?" Will spoke above the noise, his head poking over his sister as he searched the room. "I am to play chaperone tonight until my aunt arrives to guide these young women. These ladies need a man's steadying hand. Two would be better."

"You'll not put a damper on our fun, Will." Emma pouted prettily and fixed her gold mask. "I plan to make mischief and neither you nor Mama nor Aunt Ophelia can stop me."

Will Hastings grimaced at Jonas. His baleful visage saying, *See what I must contend with?* before checking the room again. His chin jutted at an empty table in a back corner.

"Ah, there's a table."

The five-some threaded past seated revelers rocking back their chairs on two legs. Evergreen boughs decorated with red bows lined heavy-wooded rafters. Tallow candles burned from wall sconces and a rustic, iron lantern lit with a dozen candles hung overhead, yet the public house was dim inside. Jonas set his hand on the small of Livvy's back and the end of her long braid brushed his hand. She'd wrapped her hair in black silk from her nape to the feathery tip swishing against her breeches.

He bent low and whispered in her ear, "A housebreaker...an excellent choice of costume."

Her head angled toward his. "I thought you would find humor in it."

His hand brushed her bottom. "You are a fast one, Livvy Halsey."

She jumped, her gaze sparkling at him like brown fire in her black lace mask.

"If ever there was a woman in need of a man's steadying hand," he teased.

Her slender nostrils flared and she almost collided with the shepherdess serving wench. Jonas grabbed Livvy's arm and pulled her close. "Careful."

The side of her body wedged up against him. Another passerby jostled them. Livvy's face was within kissing distance, but a mild storm clouded her eyes.

"You are a confusing man, Jonas Braithwaite."

"How?" he asked not liking the sharpness of her tone.

"That first night you kissed me like..."

"Like what?"

He leaned in, the balls of his feet pressing hard on the plank floor, his body on tenterhooks. Her hips fit in the notch between his legs, almost touching his placket. Any other evening, this would be unseemly, but debauchery's patina colored the Sheep's Head. People crowded close. None noticed them. Masked women landed in the laps of male patrons who caressed skirt-covered thighs. Jonas would caress Livvy's thighs, if she'd let him. But not here.

Her brows furrowed in her mask, the bottom of those copper arches visible in the eye holes. "The first night you kissed me as if I were the first and last woman for you."

"I aim to please."

"Yet the next day in the tower? It was awful. Embarrassing to say the least. Now you pat my bottom like some lascivious sailor," she finished, her lips pinching with distaste.

His mouth opened, but no words came. He'd seen lascivious sailors and his touch was a far cry from their handling of a woman's bottom. But, Livvy had a point. What could he say? That he was taken aback at her kiss last night but, tonight, he hungered for her? That he was baffled by the rush of emotions being with her?

He lightened his grip on her arm. "You have that effect on me."

The line of her mouth firmed. He wanted to erase it with a melting kiss better than what he gave her his first night home.

"I have been here a handful of days. I couldn't wait to leave. Yet, being with you is...is different."

"*How* different?"

"Braithwaite. Miss Halsey. Are you coming?" Will Hastings waved from a table squeezed between two high-back pine settles.

Jonas began to maneuver around laughing patrons. Livvy's hand on his sleeve stopped him.

"Tell me. How different?" The exposed half of her face tensed with anticipation.

He wasn't good at baring his soul. Never had been. Emotions were best kept in check.

Staring into Livvy's expectant, *hopeful* eyes, he'd swear the ground moved. His first time at sea was like this. Lightness in his stomach. The world unsteady. Yet, the ship had cut through uneven water, the sea's vastness stretching before him. It could've swallowed him whole. Instead, it became the world he needed to reach beyond simple existence and thrive. Livvy Halsey was quickly becoming the same to him—her essence was his future, his life.

That future could never be his if he didn't risk the first step with her.

"You are the kind of a woman a man could spend forever with, and forever still wouldn't be enough time with you." Shoulders squared, he smiled at her, the lightness filling him.

And by the glow in her eyes, it filled Livvy, too.

Patrons jostled around them. Her hand slid down his sleeve into his hand as if made for it. Mr. Meakin strummed notes on his fiddle, and calls for clearing the room for a dance were shouted to the rafters. Hastings called for them again.

"Come," she said, giving his hand a gentle nudge. "We have the whole night ahead of us."

He was tongue-tied as they scooted into the pine settles with the Hastings and Lady Rowena.

"What a squeeze." Lady Rowena laughed above the noise.

Miss Hastings set both elbows on the table, blowing an errant curl falling across her eyes. "Dancing and games are sure to start soon."

"What kind of games?" her brother asked, waving over a tavern maid.

Miss Hastings rested her chin in her palm. "Blind Man's Bluff for one." Her gaze wandered to the tall figure dressed as King Henry the Eighth and the Welsh archer beside him.

Lady Rowena's shoulder bumped Miss Hastings. "Because you want *him* to find you."

Miss Hastings turned a shade of pink which was a feat in their shadowed corner of the public room.

"Who is *him?*" Will Hastings twisted around in his seat. "The man dressed as King Henry the Eighth?" He turned back, scowling at his sister.

A frizzy-haired woman wearing a white mask approached the table, five cups of mulled cider clutched in both hands.

"Here you go, luvs." She leaned in and set mugs on the table, stopping herself mid-bend. "Well now, is that a Braithwaite lad come home?" She straightened and, hip cocked, set a hand on the settle's back near Livvy's head. "Bless me, it is."

Five hands reached for their cups. Jonas took his, a smile creasing his face.

"Molly Fowler?"

"The very same," she said in her throaty voice. "But it's Mrs. Molly Bainbridge now." She jerked her head at the bar where Mr. Bainbridge ran a hand over his bald pate, eyeing a daunting row of tankards in need of filling. "Married to that one which makes me proprietress to this grand place."

"That would make sense with your costume."

She showed goose down angel wings stitched into the back of her gown. "You mean an angel, masquerading as a serving wench." She laughed heartily, her gaze landing on his gold earring. "And you must be the pirate in black velvet setting all the female hearts aflutter. Our new serving maid, the shepherdess, says she'll not be the same for the sight of you."

Jonas grinned into his mug of mulled wine. Mrs. Bainbridge winked at the seat crammed with Livvy, Lady Rowena, and Miss Hastings.

"One of you fine girls could end his wanderer's ways and see him leg-shackled." She patted Jonas's arm. "This round of drinks is on me and Mr. Bainbridge. Call it a welcome home." And she shoved off, her angel's wings bobbing.

Will Hastings raised his cup. "Let us drink to a good leg-shackling. It cannot happen fast enough to my sister."

"You men get all the fun." Miss Hastings snorted delicately and set the cup to her mouth. She barely swallowed her wine before raising her cup for a toast. "I say we drink to the ladies having fun tonight."

Cups clinked and Miss Hastings raised her cup again. "And a toast for Miss Olivia Halsey who came down from her tower tonight. May one of Plumtree's fine men rescue her once and for all."

"I don't need a man to rescue me. I like what I do in my family's tower, thank you very much."

"Dusting off old Roman sandals a farmer plowed up?" Will pulled a grim face. "No thank you."

"You would say that," his sister teased. "Because your shoes have a distinct odor."

"Humph." Hastings shrugged off the minor insult by downing more mulled wine.

"Making sense of what we dig up, studying them, and putting those discoveries into words appeals to me." Livvy gulped her wine, quickly adding, "Helping my father, I mean."

"I read your father's last book, Miss Halsey. I found it quite fascinating." This from Lady Rowena before she dipped into her cup.

Livvy, warmed by the compliment, met Jonas's gaze across the table. He raised his cup in a silent toast to her skill with words.

Miss Hastings peered at her female bench-mates. "All this talk of the past does us no good, ladies. We are firmly in the present and desperately in need of fun and frivolity."

Livvy fanned herself with her hand as if about to swoon. "I wouldn't mind a night of flirtation with one of the fine gentlemen here."

Lady Rowena giggled and clinked her cup with Livvy's. "Why Miss Halsey, you are a divine creature."

Jonas gulped his wine. Livvy never fanned herself a day in her life. Not the girl he knew. But, she was a woman now—a woman he had no claim over. Nor could he say how much she'd changed these ten years. A handful of days in Plumtree wasn't enough to learn the woman she'd become.

"Careful, ladies. Remember who you are," Will cautioned, giving his sister the stern eye.

"Oh, Will," she cooed. "Be a good chaperone and fetch more mulled wine for us all."

Jonas got up and Hastings scooted free of the bench. He sat down again as Miss Hastings planted both palms on the table. She bent forward like a conspirator, speaking to Lady Rowena and Livvy with a comical, red wine moustache at the corners of her mouth. Her gaze honed in on the tall Welsh archer.

"Mr. Fortham is mine."

Jonas traced his cup's handle, waiting for the dancing to start. He'd sweep Livvy into the fun. For now, he'd endure Miss Hastings's mooning over the Welsh archer.

"There's something very…" she sighed. "Oh, I don't know. He flirted with me when he came to repair the gate at Hastings Hall. I was out for a ride and well…we had an *interesting* conversation."

Jonas idly tapped his cup on the table.

"Then, I took my horse into the village to be shod. Mr. Fortham is quite...quite..."

"Handsome," Lady Rowena supplied.

"Primal."

Livvy? Jonas's head snapped up. All eyes were on Livvy. She rolled her shoulders, one corner of her mouth curling like a freshly-sated courtesan.

"Mr. Fortham is a man of good character. He has that to recommend him," she said, tilting her cup, inspecting the spice dregs at the bottom. "He is strong and capable in mind and body."

Miss Hastings's eyes narrowed. "Pray tell, Miss Halsey, when did you learn how strong and capable he is?"

"When he came to fix the door on Halsey Tower." Livvy sipped the last of her mulled wine. "I thought common laborers were beneath you."

"A dalliance isn't out of the question. But, you can't have entertained a flirtation with him. You're promised to another man."

"To whom?" Jonas blurted the question.

Three pairs of feminine eyes turned on him as if they'd forgotten he was there. At least two of them had. Livvy's chin dipped. No, she hadn't forgotten he was there. Jonas never pretended to have full knowledge of women. Far from it. He'd had many a conversation with his previous employer and friend, the Earl of Greenwich, about the mysteries of women. Their bodies were a map he could master. But a woman's heart? Her mind? These were riddles better men than he should master.

Until Livvy.

Her brown eyes shuttered within the black lace as if she'd not answer. But, Miss Emma Hastings would. She supplied the answer to Jonas like a shark smelling blood in the water.

"Oh, didn't you know? Miss Halsey is betrothed to a Mr. Alistair Haggerty of London." Miss Hastings neatly pinned her rival for the blacksmith's affection. Jonas's gut clenched. The words delivered a hard blow. His fist curled on his thigh. He had no hold on her, but Livvy had the grace to wince.

"Here we are." Will Hastings set five cups of mulled wine on the table.

Four hands grabbed a mug and each person took their fill.

"Mr. Bainbridge tells me they'll clear the floor for dancing in five minutes." Will made to sit down.

"Wait." Jonas slid off the bench. He emptied his mug and set it down with a firm *thunk.* "I'll leave you to your fun."

"You're leaving me to be the sole guardian of these three?"

Jonas tore off his mask, stung to the core. What did he expect after one kiss and a few visits to her tower? That Livvy would swoon for him? He shouldn't have come here tonight and waited like a besotted fool for her. And he certainly shouldn't have told her how she affected him.

"You're a better man than me," he said, dropping a shilling on the table. "I'm sure you'll manage."

Chapter Six

J ONAS SHOULDERED HIS way through the crowd. Livvy scrambled off the bench and pushed up on tiptoe to see Jonas cut a wide swath to the door. He was leaving?

"Miss Halsey?" Lady Rowen's voice came from behind her.

"Don't worry about me. I'm walking home."

"Miss Halsey, I say that's unacceptable..." Will Hastings's voice faded behind her as she waded through a tide of revelers rising from their chairs. Men scraped tables across the room to stack them against the wall. It was impossible to break through the mass of people and tables and chairs.

She'd not get to dance with Jonas.

Masks swarmed around her. People laughing and drinking and hefting the Sheep's Head's tables and chairs. The din was painful to her ears. She stepped to the right and a jovial Mr. Fortham banged into her, a pint sloshing in his fist.

"Miss Halsey? Is that you?" he asked.

Heart pounding, she ducked around him fast and spoke over her shoulder. "Good to see you, Mr. Fortham."

Two burly farmers who didn't bother with masks or costumes blocked her path. She dove around them in time to see Jonas shut the inn's door behind him.

Why did that closed door feel so...*final*?

That bit about Mr. Fortham was beneath her. She'd wanted to have fun, to have Jonas dance attendance on her. His caress to her bottom had shocked her. It was more than she expected. Elbows jabbing her, she stood arms at her side, people swarming the room.

Tonight was a the rare evening when Plumtree's folk mixed, all the classes from this district to neighboring areas. Most came for frivolity. Some came for a taste of local debauchery.

She wanted both. With Jonas.

Mrs. Bainbridge sidled up to Livvy, a rag in one hand, five pints clutched in the other. "Now there went the best man in three districts. A man of solid character and—" Her throaty voice dropped suggestively "—easy on the eyes. You'd do well with the likes of him."

"He is a fine man, but I'm, I'm unofficially betrothed," she said, speaking above the clamor. "It's a business arrangement. My family duty. Friendship is all that Jonas and I have."

"*Humph!* Did the good Lord put Adam and Eve together for commerce?" The proprietress fisted the rag on her hip. "A business arrangement makes cold comfort in the marriage bed. Take it from me, you'll want a man to keep you warm at night. Should that man be a best friend? Well, *that* woman should count herself lucky."

"But Jonas doesn't want to stay in Plumtree."

Mrs. Bainbridge groaned. "All men need their minds changed. It's the first lesson of marriage, luv. Convince your blue-eyed pirate to stay and, if you can't, go with him."

She balked. "Leave Plumtree?"

"Come now, you've never been missish. There's a whole world out there. You ought to know that from helping your father."

True. She was bold in every other aspect, yet when it came to Jonas, her heart thudded and her legs stuck in place. Behind her, the room was cleared. Fiddle music hummed the first notes of a reel. Shoes scraped the floor as men and women lined up.

"Do you want him?" Mrs. Bainbridge asked.

"I do."

"Then don't stand there like a lost lamb." The proprietress shooed her away. "Go after him."

She rushed to the door and snatched her cloak off the hook. Throwing open the door, horses and dog carts cluttered the village road outside. A few coachmen tarried in the cold by finer vehicles, hands cupped over their mouths. The skies were clear, a thousand stars glimmering from heaven.

Where was Jonas?

She ran to the middle of the road and spun around. She hadn't asked how Jonas came to the inn. By horse? One of the carts? Or did he borrow the Captain's flat cart once used to deliver furniture?

Hooking the frogs under her chin, she called out to the coachmen. "Pardon me, gentlemen, have you seen a tall man in black exit the inn?"

"A big gent." The coachman tapped his ear. "Had a gold earring right here?"

"Yes, yes! That's him."

A lanky arm stretched to the east end of the road. "He went that away, miss."

She barely said her thanks before grabbing handfuls of her cloak, her legs pumping hard. She sprinted up the road, leaping over deep ruts. Tight stays manacled her ribs. There was nothing ladylike and proper about her mad dash through Plumtree. The main road curved east with a fork heading north to Halsey and Braithwaite land. She took the northern turn, and it was there she spied Jonas, his stride eating up the road. Blast it, but he was fast.

"Jonas!" she yelled, her run easing to a trot until she stopped from a stitch in her side.

He halted his progress and slowly turned around. Her feet were made of lead, and her heart lurched. Lungs billowing, she let go of her cloak and smoothed it if only to occupy her hands. Jonas stayed put, all six feet and several inches of him. The brim of his hat shaded his face, yet she *felt* his blue-eyed gaze rake her from head to toe.

A shiver skipped her spine.

Was it possible a man's hostile stare could keep a woman in place?

Jonas was a good twenty paces from her, and she dare not venture any closer. Not that she could. A horrible stitch pinched her side.

"Please. Don't go." The heel of her hand pressed the cramp. "I, I want to talk with you."

Starlight touched Jonas as he put one long leg in front of the other, making his way to her. Heaven help her but, she cringed. His forbidding glare, the gold earring gleaming like a sharp point...Jonas could be a landlocked pirate bearing down on her. He stopped a few paces away, his breath huffing clouds.

"About what?"

She rubbed the pained spot harder. "I want, I want...to be with you."

"Why?"

She shut her eyes at his icy voice. Never had she known him to be this abrupt with her. She understood the distance. He was hurt. So was she. In a matter of days, years of childhood friendship sailed full speed ahead into exciting, choppy, mysterious waters.

"Because I have feelings for you, and making sense of them is easier if we have a decent conversation."

"I'm sure your betrothed wouldn't appreciate that sentiment."

"I'm sorry about that. It's an unofficial arrangement. Nothing legally binding...more of an understanding." The words tasted like paper in her mouth, bland and silly. Jonas wouldn't quibble over the status of her arrangement. The distinction of unofficial or not didn't matter; the fact of another man did.

The whites of his eyes were wide. "You weren't honest with me."

Wincing, she stopped rubbing the cramp at her waist. She deserved the pain. "I know."

"We were always honest with each other. *Always.*" Jonas turned his face to the field. "Never, as children, was it necessary to spell out the need for telling the truth."

"Because we simply were."

"Then what changed?"

Gentle laughter rolled out of her. "Everything. Surely you see that? Ten years you were gone with hardly a word to those you left behind. And what happens your first night back? You kiss me!" She exhaled, blowing a wisp of hair out of her face. "I understand being your friend, at least what we had as children, but things have changed. We're different."

His mouth firmed. Light snapped like blue fire in his lapis lazuli eyes. Jonas advanced on her, dirt and snow crunching in the silence. He kept coming until she had to tip her head to keep eye contact.

He was a handsome man in daylight, the quiet, gentleman grandson of a furniture maker. Definitely the kind of man a woman could bring home to have tea with her mother. At midnight, Jonas devastated. Night caressed his features...his freshly shaved jawline, the width of his utterly kissable mouth, the sin-black hair falling around his face. He was an adventurer, dashing in a stoic fashion, a man of secrets and foreign places.

"I should've told you everything when I was in your bedchamber," she said, forcing her arms to stay at her sides. Otherwise, she'd touch him.

Saying aloud *when I was in your bedchamber* had an erotic effect, teasing the skin between her legs. Jonas's brows arched. Were the words an aphrodisiac to him?

"But you kissed me and that changed everything." Her voice was a wisp of sound on the empty road.

Jonas chuckled low and slipped his hand along her jaw. Black lashes hooded his beautiful eyes as his palm cupped the side of her neck. She sucked in hungry breaths. She needed him to say something, but Jonas was a man of few words, seemingly content to touch her.

"And then I kissed you when you came to my tower. An awful kiss. I was embarrassed," she said, staring at his chin, her breath hitching. "I thought you had satisfied whatever lust or curiosity about me the first night, and well...my kiss *was* bad."

"No it wasn't." His hand curled around her nape, warm and comforting. "Even a bad kiss with the right woman is heaven to a man."

Oh, that melted her...those words said in his deep voice as his strong hand caressed her neck. Pleasure shot to her toes. Her body was flush to his.

He chuckled again and the rumble stroked her insides.

"That bad kiss? I made myself not respond. I had to know what was happening with you." He kissed the crown of her head. "It's my fault. I touched you when I had no business doing so."

Waves of gooseflesh spread under her stays, the tickle skipping like pebbles down to her inner thighs. Words stuck in her mouth. Jonas's fingers slipped into her hair before tracing her spine with painfully good slowness to the middle of her back. Her forehead rested on his velvet waistcoat, and she gripped the open ends of his outer black wool coat.

How far down would his hand travel?

Jonas stroked her velvet cloak, the hush of his hand the only sound on the empty lane. She pushed up on her toes, all the better to drink him in. His shirt smelled faintly of cedar, likely from his cedar-lined sea chest. An exotic soap-scent clung to his smooth jawline. She was lost in Jonas, his hand on her body, the still road, the excited flutter in her heart that he might...might—he *did* palm her bottom cheek.

She sucked a lungful of air. His big, beautiful hand rested right there.

Where else would he touch?

Jonas hugged her and spoke above her ear, his voice thick. "I want you to listen carefully to what I'm going to say. Know that whatever you decide, you will always be my friend, one of the best memories in my life." He paused. "Give me a sign you understand what I'm saying."

"Uh-huh," she mumbled, nose deep in his cravat.

"I want to undress you. I want to kiss every inch of your skin until your voice is hoarse from crying out with satisfaction. We won't think about the future or the past. We'll be a man and a woman for—"

Chapter Seven

"TAKE ME TO the tower," she said.

"—for one night."

Heat flooded his nether regions. He pushed Livvy's shoulders back, needing to see her face. Did she know what she agreed to? Copper-colored lashes drooped over exotically tilted eyes. The full bow of her upper lip tempted him, the middle nub of her top lip inches from his mouth. He'd suck on it. Gently. And taste her...though he dare not say that. There was a hint of innocence in all her sauciness.

Yes, Livvy needed a thorough kissing, begged for it, her body swaying against him like a shameless tart. A definite *yes*.

But her answer was too quick.

Logic and lust warred inside him. They were friends. Nor could he ignore that Livvy had consumed mulled wine tonight, and she was promised to another. Unofficially, of course. His mouth opened and shut, the chance for words crumbling when Livvy's hands slipped inside his coat. She rubbed his chest, the whisper of skin on silk the only sound between them. Teeth clenched, desire surged hot and fast when she pushed his wool coat wide open. She took stock of his clothed chest, devouring him.

"Livvy...you're sure?" he asked, his voice hoarse. "About the tower?"

Curious hands traced the dip between his heavy chest muscles. "There's little room for interpretation when a man says 'I want to undress you' followed by a promise to kiss every inch of my skin."

Fingers digging into her velvet clad shoulders, he stifled a smile. He was a cad twice over for propositioning a promised woman on a country road. His stay in Plumtree would soon end. He had no prospects, no will to stay, and he was jealous to boot. He wanted to crush the man who asked for her hand.

What he wanted made no sense, but he was in no position to fish for motive and reason. His brain absorbed lust for a certain redhead the way a sponge soaked water.

"What I said was pure desire of the flesh." His voice was strained. "I didn't think."

"I don't want you to think. I want you to feel…to speak freely with me."

Speak freely? When he was always guarded? His carnal proposition had popped out, spoken from his heart or, more accurately, from his loins.

"A true gentleman would see you safely home to the bosom of your family."

Livvy's smile curled like a sated cat. "The tower is closer."

He groaned. Pleasure numbed his brain and shot straight to his stones. He breathed in her fragrance, a hint of vinegar from her toils and rose-scented soap. Did her skin taste like rose petal jam? She was supple against him, her shoulders pliant under his greedy hands rubbing her. The velvet teased his palms; her bare skin would be softer.

Two of Livvy's fingers drew a painstaking line down the middle of his waistcoat. "One…two…three—"

"Have you considered that the mulled wine has dulled your better judgment?"

Silky brown eyes smirked at him. "We can stay out here in the cold or you can trust me. It's your choice," she said. "Four…five…six—"

"What are you doing?"

"Counting the buttons I must undo to get you out of your waistcoat." Her hand stopped above his navel and her gaze met his. "Will you believe me when I get to your breeches and count the buttons on your placket?"

His stones heard that. They clenched inside his smalls.

Laughing low, he turned around and crouched low. "Get on my back."

She jumped on and slipped both arms over his shoulders, her voice light. "You're carrying me to the tower."

Jonas hooked both hands under her knees and began the hike. He'd carried her home in the same manner when she'd twisted her ankle chasing a butterfly. Was she eleven years old then? Twelve?

Livvy nuzzled his ear. "I was hoping you'd toss me over your shoulder. It's what a pirate would do."

His step faltered on a rut. Her voice, rich as warm chocolate, tickled him. She wiggled, pressing her breasts against his back, and his traitorous brain flashed images of a man's shirt stretched across sumptuous breasts when Livvy was in his bed his first night home.

"I'll pretend you're a lusty pirate, then," she said, oblivious to her effect on him.

He forced himself to focus on the toes of his boots. "Sorry to disappoint, but I was an honest sailor. If it helps, I did grow a beard and braid it in three parts for a time."

"I would have loved to have seen that."

"It was a passing fancy."

"And your employer, the Earl of Greenwich, tolerated such an appearance?"

"Lord Edward isn't your typical nob. Doesn't care about appearance or status," he said, trudging up the road, the flesh heavy between his legs.

Plumtree was pristine and white, a wintry purity. Livvy was warm at his back, a welcome burden. Would it matter to her that he'd never captained a ship? Or that the highest position he'd achieved was man of business in service to an earl? He'd seen the world as a law-abiding man, worked with his hands, the same hands he'd use to pleasure Livvy.

Bed sport leveled a man and woman...two naked bodies lost in hot, grinding sex.

He hugged her knees tighter. Being with Livvy would be nothing of the sort, and it scared him, made his heart thud. He'd tupped women, but this night with Livvy wasn't a tup. Slow, deep tenderness or frenzied passion, there was much to explore with her—and this one night for it.

Her lips moved against the shell of his ear. "Why did you go by the name Jonas Bacon after you left Plumtree? Were you a naughty man in London?"

Quivers danced on his nape. He could get used to her whispers. "Not much to tell."

Cold-hot sensations rattled inside him. He put one muddy, snow-covered boot in front of the other. Livvy wanted more than fleshly pleasure. She wanted his secrets. What she asked came with torturous emotions, the kind that ripped a boy's heart in two and molded him into a stoic man. He was good at keeping people at arm's-length, a skill he'd first mastered when slurs followed him as a boy, spoken behind his back.

Bastard. Mongrel. Baseborn.

Followed by *Big Ox. Big Oaf. And Brainless Beast* said to his face.

The roof of Halsey Tower rose in the distance. He pushed onto the side of the road and stood before an elevation. There was no fence marking the Halsey meadow save the slight rise in the soil.

"Your family's property."

"Jonas?" Livvy slid down his backside.

He stepped over the rise and, turning around, he waited for Livvy. She stayed on the roadside, midnight bathing her set chin and wide-open eyes. He knew the look. It was common to the fair sex when they required a man's answer.

"Are you avoiding answering me? Why did you go by the name Jonas Bacon in London?"

Snow lightened the darkness around them, the frozen bits spar-kling like diamonds. London was a byword on his journey since leaving home. In it was the answer to his past and his future. London's ships took him far away. Plumtree hemmed him in.

Except for Livvy. She was freedom itself with her copper hair and forward nature.

Her head tilted at a gentle angle. He caressed her jaw, the fur of her hood tickling the back of his hand.

"You're not content for sex alone, are you?"

She cupped her hand over his. "I would have *you*."

Throat dry, he swallowed hard. Her tenderness healed the edges of his sadness.

"What did you find in London?" she asked.

Denying a woman's request for intimate knowledge was one thing. Denying Livvy was another. She was a friend, a childhood memory come to life as a woman full grown who knew and saw too much, a woman who could read unspoken words in his eyes. But, she wanted him to rip out his heart and give it to her. She'd be content with nothing less.

His hand fell away from her. "You won't budge until I give you something."

Until I give you all of me.

Her silent nod was his answer. From his side vision, he spied faint smoke streaming from her tower. The squat turret was easily a hundred paces, yet the distance could be forever. Chill air braced him, cooling his ardor.

"When I left Plumtree, I was never going to come back. My mother was shamed, and the Braithwaites were upstarts." He sucked in a deep breath. "Setting fire to the Captain's furniture shop—"

"Was an accident. You can't keep blaming yourself for that. The Captain doesn't. I know that for a fact."

"It was still fuel to the fire that I was the ne're-do-well Braithwaite. Jacob was at St. Mary's College by then. I was Big Ox, remember?" He met her fixed stare with a hard one of his own.

"Big Ox bothers you. When we were children, you'd toss a jest back at them or turn away. But, tonight, you stood there and took it. *Why?* You could've told Will Halsey not to call you that."

"Because the Will Halseys of the world aren't worth the effort."

"You mean to keep it all in," she huffed. "Be a man, endure, and all that folderol."

He smiled when she stepped into the meadow, using the Captain's favored word.

"I am a man of few words. Jacob did most of the talking when we were lads. You know that."

She toed a chunk of icy snow. "Who talks for you now?"

"I do well enough."

It'd be easy to admit his size spoke for him. How often did he step into a room to men sitting up taller, shifting in their seats? To women giving their appraisal of his size? Might spoke when it was needed. Or he spoke rarely at all.

Speaking his heart and mind...he wasn't fluent in that language. The idea was akin to wearing a poorly-sewn coat, the fit awkward.

"To be a man of few words has its merit." Livvy linked her arm with his. "But sometimes, a man must speak what's in his heart."

"Other parts of me want to have their say tonight," he teased.

Livvy bumped into him, her giggle sweet in the chilly air. They strolled through the meadow, their boots sinking ankle-deep in snow. Lust was a low hum between them. Comfortable, casual, at ease, this conversing with a woman he'd undress in a matter of minutes. Was this what happened when a man was about to have sex with a woman he counted as friend? Moments ago on the road, carnal need consumed him. His cock was heavy, hidden behind his placket, hungry to slide between Livvy's thighs.

He could be happy, too, walking and talking at her side.

"But, why Jonas Bacon?" she prodded, her voice a gentle nudge. "The Captain knew the fire was an accident. You didn't have to change your name."

No. He didn't. He'd run off one day, leaving the briefest of notes for his grandfather. Jonas shook his head at the choices he'd made. The Captain had been his anchor in childhood, and Jonas had left him.

His heart heavy, they rounded the tower. The window was dark overhead.

"I took the name Bacon because it was my father's name."

"Oh Jonas." Her voice wobbled. Eyes shining up at him, Livvy twined both arms around his bicep.

"I was in London before I went on to the colonies where I spent much time...too much, it would seem. My speech changed. People thought I was colonial when I returned to England. I didn't correct them. I wanted nothing to do with Plumtree or the Braithwaite name."

Livvy's brows pinched together. He'd hurt her, but it was true. It was on the tip of his tongue to remind Livvy that she wanted this confessional; instead, he opened the tower door, the iron hinges singing a light squeak as they stepped inside.

"I'd journeyed to London to find out what I could about him. The Captain would never speak of the man. Nor did my mother."

"And what did you find?"

"A man named Mr. John Dean who'd sailed with him. Found him in a tavern near Wapping Wall. He choked on his ale when he saw me. Said he thought he was seeing a ghost." He touched his nape. "Years I thought I had Braithwaite hair, but my father's locks were just as black."

"Was this man you met able to give your heart some peace?"

There she was going on about his heart again. Did she want him on his knees, baring his soul?

"Peace?" He laughed, the harsh sound echoing in the tower. "My father died when his ship, the *Sussex*, sunk off the coast of Africa...the month I was born. He was an East India Company man, ironically a third mate and an adventurer. According to Mr. Dean, my father never intended to marry," he finished bitterly and shut the door.

He was no different than his father, a man of adventure, even serving as third mate. The parallel was uncanny.

Faint light from the upper floor crowned Livvy's head. She was beautiful and healing in the dank, unlit entry. They were supposed to be on the verge of an illicit interlude, yet the air changed. His admission left him icy and raw. No fire could warm his bones. The gentle slide of Livvy's hand on his arm did more to assuage the ache than any comforting words would.

"I'm sorry," she murmured.

"I should apologize to you. Talk of death isn't romantic."

"You don't need to woo me." She paused, her smile widening. "I'm the one who chased you down tonight, remember?"

Their voices were barely above a whisper. The passion diminished, but he couldn't argue with what replaced it—a tenderness, endearing and affectionate. Was this what happened when friendship forged its way into deeper waters? He could think of other places for her to touch, but if he said so, it'd be crude…a thing that never bothered him in the past when he was on the verge of coupling with a woman.

Livvy deserved better.

He lifted her hand to his lips and kissed it. "Come. Let's see if we can save the night."

Holding her hand, he led her up the narrow stairs behind him. Shoes scraped stone. A new thrum pulsed inside him, not so frantic and needy but no less heavy in his loins. Livvy's bare hand folded with his, the intimacy a treasure. There was no need for empty promises or false flattery. Livvy was his friend. She already knew the truth about him.

It was all very…comfortable.

They breached the upper floor, both eyeing the lone bed near the window. Rumpled sheets invited them to make a bigger mess. Embers glowed in one fireplace, the sole source of heat. He marched to the hearth and bent to stoke a fresh fire.

"Don't. The smoke. It might alert others." Furtive lashes dropped over Livvy's eyes.

Others. Meaning her family, secure in the belief that she was dancing country reels and taking a much deserved respite in the Sheep's Head. He rose from the hearth, his gaze shifting to the floor. He'd stood near this spot and assured Mrs. Halsey that her daughter's honor was safe with him.

Tonight, he'd plunder it.

Livvy set a hand on the back of a chair and toed off one boot. "We'll keep our clothes on for warmth."

"A practical solution but less satisfying," he said, dropping his hat on the table. "I'm sure you'd prefer skin to skin."

Livvy's laugh was skittish. "Skin to skin. Yes, of course." Her boot landed with a thud.

Slipping free of his coat, his palms were damp and limbs stiff. He could be blundering his way through his first time with a woman. Livvy was no better. She fumbled with her cloak's frogs under her chin, filling the room with aimless chatter.

"I'm acquainted with the buttons on your waistcoat. Thirteen of them...but the bottom four are undone. The ninth button...it's near your...placket." She glanced at that part of his breeches, her fingers shaky.

"Livvy..." He squeezed her hands and held them high on her chest in a gentle grip. "Our friendship will be as true as ever."

Her eyes shined, big and brown. They stood together in the cold dark room, letting uncertainty wash over them. Being with Livvy sated him, the stillness of breathing the same air, of pleasant conversation, and the *knowing*. Only the deepest friendship gave that gift. No doubt, he wanted to slide between her thighs, but being with Livvy was its own kind of satisfaction. And, she needed gentling. Her heart fluttered a rapid tattoo under his hands. Lust had given way to tender nerves. She trembled. Gone was the confident woman who accosted him on Plumtree's northern road.

He released her hands and set them at her side with care. It took all his powers of concentration to unhook her cloak. The silken frogs were slippery in his fingers.

"You've unmanned me."

"I have?"

"I'm as nervous as you. This is a night of firsts."

She gulped, her eyes rounding. "I, I—"

"Shhh." He touched her lips. "It's not every day friends engage in sexual congress. No matter what goes on here, you are my friend. I value that more than anything."

Livvy fell against him, wrapping both arms around his waist. "Oh, Jonas…"

He cupped the back of her head and held her close. Their bond defied explanation. To call her a friend was inadequate. She was the childhood companion who never required a favor returned. She was there, always had been, wide brown eyes taking him in, her heart listening, caring. The gap between their ages had never mattered. They were the odd, youthful friendship in Plumtree that shouldn't have made sense. Yet, the connection thrived.

"Livvy, we—"

"Don't say it." Big, glossy eyes stared up at him. "Don't say 'We don't have to do this'." Feminine fingers went to work on his waistcoat. She freed one button and then another, the effort jerky. "I wanted to be the one you kissed that day you left." Her voice thinned with unshed tears. "I know I was only fourteen, but it should have been me. Not Elspeth."

He swallowed the lump in his throat. His absence these ten years hurt her deeply.

She was fierce, undoing his waistcoat buttons. Copper brows knit together. Her breaths came in fitful huffs. He didn't fight her. Orange light traced Livvy's head, catching the bright auburn hues of her bound hair. His waistcoat undone, she started on his placket, words rushing out of her.

"All these years, I had hardly any news of you." Livvy's hands grazed his erection tenting his smalls.

Air gusted out of him and he grabbed the back of a chair. Heat flooded his abdomen. His stones twitched and his tongue refused cooperation for the mad rush inside him. He should say something to redress his brash exit years ago, but the faster Livvy toiled to free him of his smalls, the less he could form coherent words.

Her frantic hands yanked up his shirt. "I thought you'd write to me at least once." Lips quivering, she sniffled softly. "But, you never did."

He drew her close. She sobbed against his chest, fisting his shirt with both hands. Years of separation and sadness, of loss and wondering poured out of her. If tears could tell a story, Livvy wrote hers against his chest. Each warm drop mended her heart while it tore apart his. Holding her racked him. He wanted her, desired her, and yes...*he loved her.*

His knees buckled. The truth thrashed him. He blinked at the dim chamber, looking but seeing emptiness. Everything hazed. His mouth wouldn't work.

Grim facts were clear...he *was* piss-poor at speaking his heart.

Sensations swamped him. Words failed him. He needed Livvy. To feel her. To taste her. Tipping her chin high, he planted the softest kiss on her mouth. It was all he could do. He coaxed sweetness from her, his lips brushing hers, a whispery touch meant to soothe her and heal the storm inside him.

"Oh, Jonas." She breathed his name. In it was contentment, the future, and a sultry promise.

Dipping low, he sucked on the plump center part of her upper lip. A taste, a nibble...a deeper suck. She moaned, swaying into him again. Welcome friction rubbed the tip of his cock, the pleasure a white hot shock to his brain. Her homespun breeches, the wool and the wooden buttons rubbed his skin. Separation was agony. He needed to seat himself inside.

He gripped her backside with both hands and hoisted her up. Livvy yelped into his mouth, wrapping her legs around his waist. They didn't break their kiss. Mouths pressed hungrily. Tongues touched. He walked, carrying her to the bed.

"Your clothes," he mumbled into her mouth and kissed a trail to her ear.

"My clothes." Livvy shivered when his lips played with her lobe. "We should slow down."

"No," he rasped.

Her fingers bumped between them. She didn't rush. She giggled when he nipped her earlobe. When his mouth ran into her formidable cravat, he growled his frustration.

A nervous titter spilled from her. "There is no rush."

"I think there is." He bit the cravat's tie and yanked it with his teeth.

Livvy inhaled a hiss of sound. The mannish waistcoat parted. A cambric shirt covered her. The cravat loose, he searched for her shirt's opening at her neck. Touching her throat calmed him. He dragged his splayed hand from her throat, to her collarbone, to the top of her chest, careful to memorize her shape. Livvy's bare skin calmed him. This was only her neck and the top of her chest. She could be the tonic a sick man prayed for. Life-giving. Sustenance of the best kind.

What would happen when he touched the rest of her?

When he thrusted into her, her naked body writhing beneath him?

His body tightened painfully at that picture.

Breasts jostled. Pale thighs clenched his hips. Her brown eyes with their slight, exotic tilt watched him under heavy lids.

Livvy removed her coat and let it drop to the floor. "I'm counting on you to keep me warm."

"I can do that."

He lifted the hem of her shirt and tucked it under her chin. Whalebone stays cinched her. His hands spanned her ribs. Slowly, he dragged his thumbs down the whalebone, tracing the ridged lines until he landed on bare skin. No shift. This was nice. He tested the curve of her pelvic bones, following the dip into the waistband of her breeches. Her skin pebbled wherever his thumbs touched.

Livvy hissed, her shirt hem slipping free of her chin. Hands shaking, she wrangled the shirt in one hand, her the lacing of her stays with the other.

"Let me," he said, brushing her hands aside.

Milk white breasts spilled over the top of her stays. He tugged the ties, working the top three tiers with impatient hands. The lacing parted and he had to stop. The valley of her cleavage showed between the lacing. He stared, slack jawed. Full, inner curves pressed inside the stays…firm and round moving each time she breathed.

He *had* to touch.

One finger slipped past the ties inside her stays and traced a pale curve.

"Your skin is finer than velvet." He was awestruck. He had to explore the inner part of her breast again and again to assure himself of the truth—Livvy was made for his touch.

The texture of her skin, the softness...

And this was one finger on one breast.

She watched him, fascinated by his hand inside her stays. The garment slumped lower on her torso until two pink-brown nipples popped to view.

"Well, hello." He grinned, his gaze locked on those two points.

The greeting was worthy of a cad. Base and obscene. He should be romantic. Instead, he honed in on the coin-sized peaks. With both hands, he twirled the tiny tips between his thumb and forefinger in barely-there circles. Breast play was an art form he'd not perfected. He liked them. Big. Small. Full and round. Or a slight curve the likes of a small dumpling. But, this was Livvy he was touching, pleasuring, if he went by her moans.

Her head was lax, tipping to one side. He kissed the exposed skin, breathing her warmth and the wash of clean rose-scented soap on her neck while his fingers circled her areolas. The tender nipples had turned a shade of raspberry.

"I could do this all night," he said and dropped a kiss on her breast.

Livvy shuddered, a high, thin wheeze hissing from her. Her mouth went slack and a blissful hum tripped out of her again. She gaped at him. Tried to focus but her eyes were dark pools. Livvy grabbed the bottom of his waistcoat. Skin around her eyes tightened. Her face flushed and she breathed faster. Was she on the verge of finding her pleasure?

Her brown eyes begged him not to stop.

"Good, isn't it?" He gloated. He couldn't help it.

"Uh-huh."

She was his puppet and he was the marionette master...all managed from gentle circles on her nipples. His erection poked out of his breeches. He itched to be skin to skin with her, to see if the rest of her body was velvet textured, but Livvy was right. The tower was cold. They would warm each other the best they could with hot sex.

His sluggish circles on her nipples spread wider. Ripe breasts, firm as Christmas pudding flushed a shade of pink.

"Livvy."

She moaned. His hands feathered higher up her chest to her collarbone.

"Livvy." He hooked a finger under her chin, calling her out of her sensual trance. "Your breeches. Push them to your knees."

She licked her lips and tried to focus on his face. "You don't have to stop."

"I won't." He chuckled, a sense of control seeping into his limbs.

Livvy unmoored the wooden buttons on her placket. He wouldn't be surprised if she counted the number she wore too. Coppery strands of hair fell wildly around her face. She stood with a boot on one foot, a plain stocking on the other, her languorous eyes feasting on him. Not once in unbuttoning her breeches did she break eye contact.

It was potent. More than sexual congress about to happen. A primal thing.

Livvy was laying claim to him.

He didn't have to touch the seam of skin between her legs to know she was ready.

Cloth rustled. He glanced down and laughter rolled through his body. "Only you would be saucy enough to wear a man's smalls."

Could a man have it any better? Intimacy and humor with a woman. Another sign of the rightness of being with Livvy.

A satisfied smile broke her sex-hazed stare. It eased the corners of her eyes and lit up her face. "Doesn't every Englishwoman wear smalls with her breeches?"

He pulled the string holding up that intimate garment. "A question to haunt many a man, I'm sure."

She was a sight. Breeches down to her knees. Slender, naked thighs lightly muscled and pale in the unlit room. Shirt pulled up. Breasts peeking over her stays. And a dusky spot in the middle of her untied smalls. The sum total of a vision.

Playful. Sweet. Erotic.

He locked on to the thatch between her legs. "The smalls. Push them down."

His voice was gruff. He couldn't take his eyes off the juncture of her thighs shrouded in linen. Livvy hooked both hands in her smalls and wiggled her hips.

The bit of cloth dropped to her knees. For a second or two, he couldn't breathe. A steel band could be crushing his lungs. The lack of air seemed to scramble his brain. A neat triangle of auburn curls was all he could see.

"Lay down for me." The command left him taut as a fiddle string.

His skin was tight. Joints and muscles tensed. Desire wound him up.

Livvy seated herself on the bed and lay back. He bent over her, smelling her sex. His cock ached. A wet line darkened the feminine curls between her legs. He had to touch it.

One finger skimmed the dampness.

Livvy spread her knees wide, her stockinged foot freed from her breeches. Slick flesh opened for him. Fingers to her mouth, she watched him.

He stroked her hip. Words tumbled from him as he stroked every inch of her exposed skin, kissing a small bruise the size of a thumbprint on her thigh. His hand tucked under her stay, feeling the plane of her belly, the solid curve of her ribs. If he had a lifetime to touch Livvy, it wouldn't be enough. He hungered for her.

"Jonas...I..." Emotions flickered in her eyes. Things unsaid. Their history. Years of friendship. And desire.

How strong she was to be this vulnerable with him.

It made him weak in the knees.

Lowering himself, he braced one hand on the bed and held her gaze. The other hand pushed his breeches and smalls to his knees. Measure for measure. They were equals. Always had been. Entwined.

Connected. Full of secrets and memories.

This would be the best part of knowing Livvy.

He set the tip of his cock at her entrance. Her throat moved with a hard swallow.

"Do it fast," she urged and rocked into him.

Blinding heat bounced from his genitals to his brain. He cried out. The sound echoed off the tower's timbered ceiling. The shock of soft, wet skin closing tightly around the head of his cock. Her words reached through the lustful fog.

Do it fast.

"Livvy?" he croaked. His brain tried to make sense of the feeling assaulting him.

Her hips swayed into him. "Please."

Livvy was practically begging him to impale her. He was a fraction deeper inside her. Slick, feminine flesh gloved the part of him inside her.

But…

The tip of his cock touched a barrier. His forehead rested on hers as he clutched handfuls of the sheets.

"You're a virgin." His voice shook. His body shook. He fought to control himself.

A stockinged foot snaked around his waist. "Not anymore."

Livvy drove herself against him, whimpering. Her pained sob tore his heart. She grabbed his shoulders with both hands and held on tight. Her body quaked. She was panting.

"Shhh," he soothed. Livvy's hot, wet tightness was heaven for him, but it pained her. "Let your body adjust."

Her breath came in fits. "It's not so bad."

"It gets better," he said, stroking her hair.

They stayed locked together, their hearts pounding and breaths jagged. This was a night of firsts—of sex between two friends and the act itself for Livvy. His mind reeled at the implication.

She'd saved herself for him.

Nature's urges wanted him to drive into her, but they stayed together, unmoving. It was killing him. The wait. The desire marching down his spin. His ass squeezed tight. Livvy needed this moment, and he'd give it to her. Her inner muscles gave a slight clasp to his shaft as if testing the feel, experimenting with what she could do.

Air wheezed past his clenched teeth. She needed to explore and adjust to him.

The tower was cold, but a drop of sweat trickled down his back.

Livvy tucked herself against him, her breath fanning his neck. "I liked when you touched my breasts, and I liked it when you kissed me."

She pulled his hand free of its tense grip on the sheets and set it on her breast.

"If I touch you more," he rasped. "It'll be harder to not move inside you."

"If you touch me more, it'll be harder for me to keep still with you inside me." She kissed his neck and wiggled her hips beneath him. "The ache is fading."

He kissed her and braced one hand on the mattress. Staring into her eyes, his free hand feathered light touches on her breasts spilling out of her stays. His other arm shook from holding himself up. Need racked his body from the sweetest pleasure-pain.

His cock was buried deep inside Livvy.

"You are a good man," she whispered, slipping her hands under his shirt.

Livvy's fingertips drew light lines on his skin before raking his skin to his navel. He shuddered. Holding still was a feat. It tested the limits of his restraint. Weakness stole up his legs.

"Livvy...I..." His gut tightened when her fingers skimmed the nest of hair above his cock.

Her quim's inner walls squeezed him again. Livvy rocked back and forth, making the bed ropes squeak. Little movements, gentle as a swaying ship. Back and forth. Back and forth.

"I like this," she whispered, pulling him closer. "I want this, more of this...more of you, Jonas."

His stones hurt and his cock ached from the waiting. But, Livvy was worth it. He ceased thinking and let his body feel. Nature was having its way between them. Need rushed him. His hips bumped against hers, rusty and imperfect. Livvy didn't seem to mind. Her hips bumped against his. The mattress creaked louder. The bed frame banged the tower wall. Faster and harder. Their breaths mingled. He rained kisses on her cheek and mouth, hungry for Livvy. There was a world of things he wanted to say, and none of them he could voice. Clarity was lost.

Passion rushed fast and hard. Livvy's blissful cries blended with his guttural moans, the purest music as they reached for their pleasure together.

The tower faded. His past and his future.

Life was this moment with Livvy. No one was going to keep her from him.

No one.

Chapter Eight

PAIN GAVE WAY to bliss. Jonas crashed into her. Or did she crash into him?

Joining with a man wasn't what she expected, this shock of emotions and sensations. Tender skin twitched between her legs. She'd be sore. The benefit of an older, once-married sister was whispered confidences of the marriage bed.

But she was not married to Jonas.

This was an assignation in her tower, fully dressed while surrounded by the smells of vinegar and Roman antiquities and dirt. The past always came with a little dirt.

Jonas lay on top of her, breathing hard and sucking her neck. Hot, wanton flares burned down to simmering spangles. Her body was alive. Was it possible sex was meant for a woman's well-being? Further exploration was necessary. A complete study to catalogue all the things a man and a woman could do to each other and the corresponding response. Her body craved more...his waistcoat's slippery silk on her stomach, her fingers combing his short hair, Jonas's earring skimming her arm. The metal was warm from their embrace. Velvet abraded her nipples. Big, hairy thighs rubbed hers. Sensations pummeled her, too many to assess properly. One feeling, though, was most curious.

"You're shrinking inside me."

Jonas laughed against her neck, the vibration as satisfying as his stones resting against her vagina. He nuzzled her earlobe and her booted heel dug into the mattress when he found a ticklish spot.

Her hips wiggled. She tested her inner muscles, squeezing him again. "Definitely softer now."

He pushed up, his smile a white crescent in the dark. "As it happens when sexual congress ends."

"I should like to do this again." She tugged down her shirt when icy air bit her exposed skin. "But with less clothes and a warm chamber."

"Have plans do you?" Gentle mirth filled his words.

Jonas withdrew from her and rose from the bed. She felt the stickiness of his seed and her sex mingling between her legs. The slickness of it.

His loss chilled her, but she was in no hurry to get up. "I liked you kissing my neck afterward. There should be more of that."

"Duly noted," he said, pulling up his breeches.

It was fascinating watching Jonas collect himself. He tucked in his shirt and didn't bother to retie his smalls. Was that a post-sex habit of his to neglect his smalls? Jonas scowled, too, when he smoothed his shirt inside his velvet breeches.

"You understand this was rushed. It all happened too quick."

She mumbled something, the words unintelligible from her finger resting on her bottom lip.

"Sex should be longer. A thing enjoyed for a night," he explained.

A man dressing was just as intimate as the undressing. With the mullioned window at his back, light outlined broad shoulders and made the gold glint on his ear. Black velvet strained to cover him, the fabric denting where his shoulder curved in to meet his bicep. Jonas had always been strong. He'd been her protector in their youth. When other village boys didn't want her along, Jonas had defended her. When raiding local orchards, Jonas would toss the choicest fruit to her with a wink. When he labored in the Captain's shop and she'd happen to stop by, he'd give her a moment and the promise of a ramble once the work was done.

She loved the smell of sawdust and wood, of ripe plums and Jonas.

Was it wise to tell a man she loved him the same night she'd confessed to being promised to another?

She covered her mouth and watched his beautiful hands button his waistcoat. He colored her childhood with fond memories. How much better and richer a future with him would be.

"We must do this again outside in the sun at the height of summer," she said wistfully.

Fingers slowing, his blue gaze stabbed her heart. Summer was out of the question. He wouldn't be here.

"Don't say it." She buried her nose into the sheets. "I forgot."

Talk of lying naked with him meant a future together. Jonas wouldn't be here past Twelfth Night. Her mouth filled with a plea for him to stay longer, but that would make her a grasping woman, especially since she was betrothed to another. She pulled the ends of her waistcoat together, tears pricking her eyes. Oh, this was lowering. Elspeth was quick to cry. *Not her!* Why, then, was this her second spate of weepiness in the same night?

Is this what happened when a woman yearned for a man? Wanting him turned her into a blubbering coil of emotions?

She would have none of it. Wiping her face, she'd not let him see these tears. They belonged to her alone. Nudging herself up, the sheets rustled a last invitation to stay put. Jonas didn't feel the same pull. Fully dressed, he plucked her coat off the floor and tossed it over his shoulder.

"Come. The first order of business is to see you home."

Chin to chest, she rose, stretching her shirt hem over her naked thighs. There had to be a better way for sex to end. Wasn't it more romantic than this? She was half-dressed but fully bared to him, as good as admitting this was more than a lustful tumble. Accepting her coat, she couldn't meet his gaze.

Jonas walked to the table for his coat and hat. "It's late."

She began putting herself together. Shirt hastily tucked in her breeches, she fixed her waistcoat. Her fingers fumbled on the straight line of buttons and button holes. The garment gapped where she'd missed two buttons.

"It'll have to do," she mumbled to herself.

The floorboards creaked with Jonas's approach. Head down to close her placket, bronze velvet swung into view. Jonas's deep voice broke the awkward silence.

"I could've made the night better had I known."

Eyeing him from under her lashes, she sealed two top buttons and left the rest undone. "If I told you I was a virgin, you wouldn't have touched me."

Mouth set, he handed over her cloak. "Probably not."

"What is it with us?" She swirled the cloak around her shoulders and raised her hood. "We're so close, yet out of reach."

His jaw muscles worked. The subtle twitch telling her he mulled this problem, too. She waited for him to say something, to share an ounce of feeling, but the truth was he showed more reaction when he was inside her than fully clothed. Jonas stood stalwart as ever, a man of few words and closely held emotions.

This should have been a momentous night. She'd given herself to the one man she truly wanted—her dearest childhood friend. Yet, the past bond wasn't enough to bridge a future together.

She sped for the stairs. Footfalls hit the floors after her. She raced down the winding staircase out to the cold. Cold midnight air burned her lungs. The back of Halsey Manor in view, she marched through the back garden aware of the male specter behind her.

"Livvy. Wait."

"You don't have to see me home. As you can see, it's right here."

She didn't regret her waspish tongue. Even the best of men needed a good set down. And for all the hurt, Jonas was still a rare man. Tonight knocked him off the pedestal. Or did she see him more clearly now? That was the rub with memories. They framed a man with the veneer of perfection. A grown woman couldn't be fanciful when considering the future—even the best of heroes had feet of clay.

And imperfect heroes persisted. At least Jonas did. His long legs cut through the snow alongside her as she rounded the manor. He didn't give up. Jonas trod the wide steps up to her front door at her side.

"There's more I want to say but not like this. Not in these circumstances."

She pulled her cloak tightly about. This was promising. Perhaps she'd been rash? A single candle lantern lit the front door, one of the minor economies of late. Her family wasn't down in the heel, nor were they as flush in the coffers as in the past. The lone candle served as a reminder she had obligations to the people she loved. They counted on her, and she counted on Jonas.

"You will come back to the tower tomorrow?"

Lapis lazuli eyes gleamed boldly at her. The rakish earring did, too.

"For the chair," she said firmly. She would not ask again to lie with him.

Jonas smiled at her, the first glimmer of friendship shining in his face. "I gave my word to restore the chair."

"Good. I'm sure we can get past this. We promised to remain friends...at least for, for however long you'll remain in Plumtree."

He stretched out his hand, palm up. She shifted from one foot to the other.

"What's this?"

"My hand," he teased. "I believe it's customary for a woman to place her hand in a man's palm when he offers it."

"I *know* the custom. There's no need for fine manners out here at midnight. No one will see."

She set her hand in his anyway. Her fingertips had gone numb, but his breath warmed her knuckles. "It's not about what others see. It's about you and me."

They'd both been remiss about donning gloves tonight. Jonas planted a chaste kiss on the back of her hand. Straightening to full height, he held her fingers longer than propriety allowed. But, they'd already dashed headlong from proper to improper in her tower.

Tenderness lit his blue eyes shaded under the brim of his hat. "I will come for you in the morning."

With that, he turned on his heel and trotted down the stairs. She stared speechless at the wide line of his shoulders. The bottom of Jonas's coat swayed with his—dare she say?—jaunty step. He trod the

Halsey drive to the north road, a whistle drifting after him.

Head shaking, she opened the door and shut it quietly. She swiped her boots clean on the boot swipe, lost in the comforting stillness of home. The clock ticking in the hall. Her footsteps sinking in the entry's thick carpet with its cream and light blue pattern. The medallion with a chip in the plaster above the cloak hooks.

And the empty chair where the housekeeper, Mrs. Tillmouth, or a footman usually waited for all to come safely home.

"I sent Mrs. Tillmouth to bed." Her mother's voice floated from the unlit hall until she came into view, her thick auburn braid rested on her shoulder like a laurel. Her eyes narrowed shrewdly. "I see you had quite an evening with Mr. Braithwaite."

"What makes you say that?" She smoothed her coat, her stance awkward. It was foolish. She was a woman of twenty-four...not far from being on the shelf.

Her mother glided into the drawing room where she beckoned Livvy to follow. "Wet boots. Your rather quiet entrance...sans the Hastings' carriage."

Livvy followed her into the drawing room, and her mother shut the double doors behind them.

"And there are your waistcoat buttons. They are not properly fastened." Her mother's continental accent was light behind her. "Or should I say re-fastened?"

She gasped, both hands covering her midsection. Her mother strode forward, her elegant, blue dressing gown swaying. She lit a taper and touched it to a brass candelabra, fine lines etching her forehead.

"As much as I should scold you for letting Mr. Braithwaite kiss you, we have bigger problems than your evening's escapades."

"Father?"

"No. Mr. Haggerty. He's here."

"Here's here *now*?" Livvy sunk into the nearest chair. The man she'd unofficially agreed to marry.

"Sound asleep upstairs thanks to Mrs. Tillmouth's tincture. He complained of a headache when he arrived. But between you and me, the good woman spiked it with one of her stronger herbs in an effort to save your hide, my dear."

"I didn't think he'd be here this soon."

Her mother poured port into a crystal glass. "Your Mr. Haggerty is most anxious to have the banns read. He brought his solicitor, Mr. Kendall."

Humph! Her Mr. Haggerty. He'd want nothing to do with her if he knew what had happened tonight. No one could tell. Not even her mother. The comment about letting Jonas have his way with ardent kisses was enlightening. That's what her mother believed had happened. Brushing hair off her face, that's what she'd let her mother keep thinking.

Livvy's shoulders sagged inside her coat. What about Mr. Haggerty? He was their best chance for the best price for the chair.

But how could he know what she'd done? Sex didn't brand a woman.

Her mother took a sip of port. "Mr. Kendall asked for a copy of the settlement deed allowing a female to inherit Halsey lands."

Livvy's heart sunk to knees. "It's happening, isn't it?"

She stared out the glass doors which opened to the garden. Snow peppered the garden's low hedges set in geometric rectangles. The keen observer could spy two sets of footprints had trailed through the simple maze, having come from Halsey Tower. The medieval structure tipped like an old friend waiting for her. Inside the stone pile, she'd given her body to Jonas. She'd given her heart, too, even if he didn't grasp what she'd done.

She'd been giving pieces of her heart to Jonas Braithwaite since she was a little girl. Her strong, silent neighbor with his sturdy shoulders and brilliant blue eyes was the one she loved.

Jonas was her hero.

"Despite his enthusiasm for the financial benefit of marriage, I do believe he has a tendre for you," her mother said quietly.

Livvy winced and locked her fingers together on her lap. If she listed the fine qualities of Mr. Alistair Haggerty, the man was a dream. Handsome, educated, a well-to-do merchant of antiquities. He treated her well and even supported her wish to write stories about Roman heroes. A perfect man in every sense, except for one—he wasn't Jonas Braithwaite.

"Mr. Haggerty insisted on going to the Sheep's Head." Her mother studied her over the crystal glass. "One can only wonder if he would've found you there."

Livvy bit her bottom lip. Her mother suspected some mischief. There were many things she could tell her mother, but what she'd done tonight was not a confessional she cared to give. The drawing room's far glass door reflected the two Halsey women, but there was also her sister to consider. Dear Elspeth. Gentle-natured, rare to venture outside Society's rules, and a widow with three children. The weight of her sister's needs bore down on her.

Marriage to an accomplished merchant benefitted everyone. Marriage to a furniture-maker's grandson only benefitted Livvy's heart—*if* he even wanted it.

A hush of footsteps sounded on the carpet and her mother was kneeling before her, folding warm hands over hers. "I see the longing in your eyes. Does your pirate feel the same for you?"

"I don't know."

Her mother hummed thoughtfully. "If a man truly loves you, if he truly wants *you*, he will declare it from the mountaintops."

Brows pinching, Livvy's bottom shifted on the cushion. "I don't know if Jonas has such mettle. He's not one for emotions, grand or otherwise."

"Then I wonder if he truly loves you," her mother whispered.

She jerked in her seat. "Mother—"

"Oh, I know he cares for you. He was always quick to look after you, but lifelong, abiding love between a man and a woman?" Her mother cossetted her hands, her voice full of passion. "He must be unafraid to declare it."

"I, I don't know…"

Motherly arms reached up and hugged her.

"Fate has not been kind to us of late. Your father's infirmity. Elspeth losing her husband. And you, toiling to save us when you should have your own life." A long sigh punctuated the silence and the hug tightened. "Promise me, Olivia, you will not be rash tomorrow. *Please.* Much rests on what you do."

Exhausted, she mumbled agreement and lost herself in the motherly embrace. Jasmine, light and spicy, scented the air. Her mother's perfume. In it was a history of understanding and tender love. Livvy was grateful her mother never prodded her into the Marriage Mart. The daughter of an antiquarian, her mother experienced firsthand the joy of historical finds. She understood it and she understood her daughters. Both of them and how different they were.

Despite recent hardships, life had been rich. But, Livvy wished for traditional things like a husband and children to warm her on cold nights.

The question was...*who would be that man?*

Chapter Nine

"**I** SIMPLY CAN'T countenance it. A settlement deed allowing a female to inherit." Paper rattled in Mr. Kendall's hand. "I can count on one hand the number of fee tail arrangements I've seen that allow such a thing."

"As you can see, everything is in order." Her mother's voice was more firm than usual this morning.

Correction. This afternoon.

Livvy glanced at the drawing room clock chiming half past twelve. She'd kept vigil at the glass door overlooking the garden, waiting for a certain blue-eyed pirate coming to call on her tower. The snow was pristine save last night's footprints...and those were melting under the bright winter sun. Azure skies rolled on forever, beautiful enough to shock a body into believing summer had come.

It all added up to a day of contradictions. Like her.

She traced a rosette in the carpet with the toe of her lavender slipper. Hair piled high and pearl earbobs dangling, she was the picture of purity in a beribboned day gown. Cream silk bows populated her person, from her chaste bodice to the split lavender and cream skirt. For goodness' sake, she was twenty-four not twelve. Wide panniers saved the gown from girlish excess. Pinching one irritating bow at her elbow, she knew why her mother requested she wear this gown. With its high cut bodice and soft colors, the gown said *youth* and *purity*.

The soreness between her legs told her otherwise.

In her vigil, polished black shoes came into view. The shoes and the well-turned calves above them were inches from her hem, a shade too close for propriety.

"Miss Halsey, are you finding these negotiations tedious?" Mr. Haggerty's voice was a silky tenor.

She met his black-eyed gaze, a pleasant frisson touching her skin beneath the pile of silken skirts. He'd said once his mother was of Portuguese descent. That explained his black hair and black eyes. Today, he wore a periwig and velvet suit a shade of port wine. Empirically speaking, her betrothed was a handsome man, a picture of refinement and sophistication.

"Why couldn't he look like a toad?"

Mr. Haggerty cocked his head. "Beg pardon?"

Her eyes rounded. "Did I say that aloud?"

"Indeed, you said something about 'looking like a toad'." The corners of his sculpted mouth turned up. "Were you referring to me?"

Cheeks prickling hotly, her mouth opened to spout polite nonsense to deter him from her faux pas, but it'd be a waste of air. The man already knew he appealed to women. No need to further stoke his ego's fire. Deflection wouldn't work either. Little slipped past Mr. Haggerty's notice. The man sniffed out charlatans on a daily basis. Buying and selling antiquities attracted all sorts. A man in his position had to be as comfortable taking tea with Europe's finest families as he did muscling his way around dockside rufflers.

It crossed her mind to ask glibly if he'd ever been a naughty man, haunting London's docks and taverns, but she bit her tongue when her mind veered to Jonas and his tale of a dockside tavern. Perhaps, maturity meant putting aside her forward nature? She ought to be elegant and demure like Elspeth.

Standing taller, she called on years of excellent breeding. "My apologies. I have been a neglectful hostess, haven't I?"

"You do seem distracted." His chin jutted at the animated discussion on the settee. "Is it the negotiations?"

Her mother listed specific household items meant for Elspeth, a line pinching above her nose. The young, fair-haired solicitor insisted on seeing the pieces before cataloging them for perpetuity. Mr. Haggerty chuckled low as the two left the room, hotly debating the valuation of Tuscan pottery.

"Mr. Kendall is a stickler for monetary details. It makes him a perfect business partner." Mr. Haggerty gave her a pained smile. "Unfortunately, it takes all the finesse out of courtship."

"I don't remember that happening. The part about courtship. Nor do I recall you saying Mr. Kendall is your business partner."

His nod was full of patience and understanding. "There is much we don't know about each other."

Her mind toyed with the idea of full disclosure, but her mother's request came to the fore. To speak plainly at this delicate juncture would be rash.

Mr. Haggerty took appraisal of her as if a new, interesting facet came to light. She imagined he gave the same subtle assessment to everything else he acquired, and make no mistake—this was an acquisition of mutual benefit. His smile widened, denting both sides of his mouth. It made her believe he'd worn a fine mask with her all morning, and now the real Mr. Haggerty was beginning to show. The beauty of his face could melt a woman except for one thing—her betrothed didn't own her heart.

Jonas did.

As each hour passed, she grew convinced of another fact. He'd deserted her.

She twisted the bow at her elbow. Bland emptiness washed over her, the same as when Jonas left ten years ago without a farewell. "Perhaps you can tell me about your business. Mother tells me you opened a shop in Bath."

"Miss Halsey, I'd be happy to share business details with you, but something tells me it would bore you to tears."

"Not at all."

He raised a placating hand. "Please. We're about to embark on a union that will change everything. The least we can do is be honest with each other."

Why did he have to be so reasonable?

"You are a good man, Mr. Haggerty."

He was also the one person in London her mother had confided in about her father's condition. He'd been helpful, buying up almost all the relics in their tower that could be restored, selling them to collectors and museums alike. In the same spirit of assistance, he'd suggested a marital arrangement. The proposition had taken her by surprise. He'd flirted with her in the past, the mild sort that sophisticated men like him did. But, she couldn't picture him growing old, doting on children, or being satisfied with a country ramble. Mr. Haggerty was a Town creature, while she was purely rustic.

"Why don't you tell me what you've been doing in your tower?"

"What I've been doing in my tower?" She winced. Repeating what the man said was worthy of a dullard. She cleared her throat. "I've been copying my father's notes for his final volume."

"What about the pieces from the Learmouth excavation?"

"Well, there is an interesting mosaic fragment, depicting a horse race in the Hippodrome."

"What about the curule chair? Your mother tells me a local furniture maker is assisting with the restoration."

She blanched. "He's doing all the work. He refurbished the hinges and saved the wood work in the chair's back rest. Not a single bead was lost in the relief carving."

"A craftsman of many years, I understand. Your mother mentioned his shop is a long-established business in Plumtree. Braithwaite Furniture and Sons."

Was her mother spinning fiction of an old man toiling with her in the tower? Mr. Haggerty didn't seem to be a jealous man. But she'd never had the chance to determine this about him, and when it came to the male mind, she was woefully uneducated.

"Mr. Braithwaite is talented. His hands are quite…skilled." She focused on the brilliant skies beyond the glass door certain her cheek burned bright red. Her mind flashed on those skilled hands playing with her nipples, but that wasn't the worst of it.

There had to be a special ring in Dante's hell for all the deceptions she'd woven of late. Penning a book in her father's name, restoring relics as if she were an experienced antiquarian, and now this small ruse about the age of the man she'd been locked away with in her tower.

"I envy Mr. Braithwaite. He must have your confidence. Otherwise you would not have allowed him into your father's inner sanctum."

"Inner sanctum?"

"The tower," he said affably. "Your father never let me inside. He didn't want me to see a piece until the restoration was complete; otherwise he feared I might decrease my offer if I saw it in a less than perfect state. Your furniture maker must know the depth of your father's infirmity. Proof of your trust in the man."

She managed a semblance of a smile. "Indeed."

Were her shoes sinking in a bog of lies?

Voices blended in the hall. Her mother and Mr. Kendall re-entered the drawing room. This time, they discussed a rare Byzantine coin Mr. Haggerty had added to his personal collection.

"Why don't you take me to the tower?" Mr. Haggerty asked.

"I couldn't." Her brain raced with how to put him off. She couldn't go back to the tower...not with the blood-smeared sheets for all to see.

His brows shot high. "Couldn't?"

Her brain raced for an idea, she said the first thing that came to mind.

"My shoes." She raised her hem a revealing inch, showing lavender silk slippers tied with cream bows.

"Something tells me those are not your typical footwear."

"Is my fidgeting giving me away?" She let go of her skirts. "Boots would've clashed with the angelic appearance."

"Most assuredly." He chuckled and formality melted with it. "You are a unique one, Miss Halsey."

"What gave me away? My discomfort in this hideous gown?" She dragged both palms over her waist. "The design belongs to a girl in the school room."

His gaze lit with male appraisal, drifting over the length of her, pausing on her high, stuffed bodice before landing on her face again. "When I dress you, it will be in vibrant colors."

Her hands froze on her stomacher.

The toe of Mr. Haggerty's shoe disappeared under her hem. He nudged her chin with one finger, the daring touch lingering while he searched her eyes.

"Yes. Bold, autumn shades, I think, with contrast trim and very little lace." His voice dropped for her ears alone. "And a low, low neckline."

"Ah." She swallowed hard. His black eyes could put a woman in a trance. "Such expertise…an unexpected benefit to have a husband know how his wife should dress."

"I will take pleasure in it."

"I am a rustic, you know. Plumtree is in my blood. I've never cared about Town or about the latest fashions."

His hand dropped from her chin to seek her hand. He lifted it to his mouth. "I wouldn't want you any other way."

And he kissed her knuckles. The same spot where Jonas planted his kiss.

"You will be my pet project," he murmured.

"Mr. Jonas Braithwaite, ma'am." Mrs. Tillmouth's announcement cut through the drawing room.

Livvy gasped, her attention snapping to the door. Jonas stared daggers at her hand resting in Mr. Haggerty's. Blood rushed from her head. Mr. Haggerty's grip tightened. Blinking at Jonas, she tried to pull her hand away, a discreet pull, a yank, followed by a heartier wrenching that finally set her hand free.

Her mother made introductions, detaining Jonas with a light touch to his arm.

"Your furniture maker," Mr. Haggerty said for her ears only.

At least Jonas wore plain blue broadcloth today. His nattier velvet attire would make convincing Mr. Haggerty of Jonas's wood-working skills nigh to impossible.

"He is the grandson of Mr. Braithwaite of Braithwaite and Sons

Furniture Company," she said quietly. Or was it Braithwaite Furniture and Sons? Her pulse pounded in her ears, and her face felt hot.

"And you toiled *alone* with him in your tower?"

"I had little choice."

Mr. Haggerty hummed his doubts, an air of formality cloaking him again. It had to be his armor in the world. Despite it, he seethed with jealousy, taking in the gold earring and leather breeches as Jonas made his announcement.

"I've come to work on the chair." But his eyes were on Livvy, saying *I've come for her.*

Yet, he was silent. Where was the bold man of last night?

"I do not think you needed to come to the drawing room to an-nounce that," Mr. Haggerty said. "The servant's entrance would have been more appropriate."

"Mr. Braithwaite is a longtime friend of the family's." Her mother actually took a half-step between the men, her voice modulated. "We all owe him a debt of gratitude for the work he's done on the curule chair."

"It's true," Livvy put in. "If it had been me, the hinges would've disintegrated. Half the bead carvings lost and the chair's arched back rest split in two."

Mr. Haggerty stood taller beside her, glaring across the room. "That talented are you?"

Jonas's eyes burned a shade of cobalt. "A deft hand, the right amount of lubricant...yes. I have a care with everything I touch."

She wanted to crumble on the spot. Jonas was a touch crude. Her betrothed bristled beside her while Mr. Kendall coughed politely in his balled fist. She wasn't an expert at sexual things, but that sounded a little off and highly charged with innuendo.

Swallowing hard, she said, "We shouldn't keep Jo—uh, Mr. Braithwaite from his work."

"We're *all* counting on him," her mother put in, a fine reminder they needed him.

Mr. Kendall sat down on the settee and shuffled papers. "We won't keep you from your work, then."

Her mother smiled benignly, both hands clutched at her waist.

"I'll have to go with him." Livvy's gaze shot from Mr. Haggerty to her mother and Jonas. "To let him into the tower. It's locked."

Did her shoes sink deeper into the carpet's pile? She imagined Dante's circle for liars expanding again for her and the colossal mistruth she'd just said. Her mother's knuckles turned white against her plum silk skirts, and Jonas, well, her pirate simply smiled easily for the first time since entering the drawing room. The tower door hadn't been locked in years.

"Yes. He certainly can't repair the chair in here, now can he?" her mother said smoothly.

"If you'll excuse me, gentlemen, Mother." Livvy snatched handfuls of her odious, beribboned skirts and scurried for the doorway.

"Olivia, don't tarry over your father's notes," her mother called after her. "We have our guests to attend."

Her heels clicked fast on the entry. Her shoes. She couldn't trounce through the snow in a perfectly good pair of silk slippers. She snatched her black wool cloak off the hook.

"We'll have to take the servant's door."

"The servant's door," Jonas grated. "Is that for his benefit?"

No need to say whose benefit. Mr. Haggerty stood at the epicenter of the drawing room, arms crossed tightly, an elegant scowl on his face as he watched her and Jonas in the entry hall.

"No. It's for mine," she hissed, her gaze darting to Mr. Haggerty. "My boots are there. Mrs. Tillmouth noticed they needed a good cleaning after last night."

"Because you were with me." Jonas slipped into his coat.

"Exactly." Keeping her voice low, she marched off to the kitchen. There was nothing graceful about her charge.

Jonas lumbered silently beside her, but he gloated. She'd seen the same expression on his face when he'd bested other village boys in summer foot races or fisticuffs. But, this was not a game, nor was she a prize to be won.

"I may as well have announced to the entire household I was not at the Sheep's Head. If I was, the mud from Plumtree's roads wouldn't have been on my boots," she said under her breath while pushing into the kitchen. "Because I was chasing down a certain stubborn man."

Mrs. Tillmouth sipped a dish of tea at the kitchen table, the household account book open before her. "Mr. Braithwaite, Miss Olivia. How nice to see you."

Mrs. Malcolm, the cook, wiped her hands in her apron, beaming at Jonas from her place by the stove. "Bless me! I'd heard the young Mr. Braithwaite was back in Plumtree. Now that I've clapped eyes on you, I'll bake your favorite biscuits. You always had the heartiest of appetites." Her apple cheeks deepened as she added, "And what a fine, strapping man you've become."

"Thank you Mrs. Malcolm, Mrs. Tillmouth. It's good to be home."

Mrs. Tillmouth set down her tea. "Rumor has it you're not long for Plumtree. Are there more fascinating adventures ahead?"

"At present, ma'am, I'm bound for the tower. It's both fascinating and an adventure in there."

"You sound just like Miss Olivia and her father, bless the man." The housekeeper tittered. "I had hoped you would rescue Miss Olivia from that pile of stones."

"He's working on the Roman chair that was delivered from the Learmouth excavation," Livvy said. "I'm to show him something, and I need my boots."

"Of course. Your mother told me about Mr. Braithwaite helping the family. A good thing he learned at the Captain's side all those years. A fine trade, furniture making." Her smile sparked with mischief as she looked to Livvy. "Your boots are on the back step. I had to take a brush to them."

Did the whole household know she was up to no good? Livvy led Jonas through the kitchen to the servant's door. She grabbed a ring of keys off a hook. Jonas cocked his head when she dropped them into her pocket.

"The tower *does* have a lock. It's rusted and hangs behind the door."

"We wouldn't want your Mr. Haggerty to have any doubts," he said as she swept outside the servant's entrance.

Mr. Haggerty's snipe about the servant's door stung and, no doubt, the swipe struck a blow to Jonas. Growing up, she and Elspeth took the servant's entrance when they came home from a ramble, their shoes dirty from a summer day's adventure. Their friends had done the same, stealing Mrs. Malcolm's warm biscuits from the kitchen table.

Her mother and father had acted as tutor when they were young. It wasn't until both girls were older that a governess came to the Halsey household. The sole purpose of the governess was to instill decorum and teach French. For Livvy, the latter was a dismal failure. The former was, too.

Wrung out and exhausted, she plopped down on the wet bench beside her boots drying in the sun. "I missed you this morning."

Jonas donned his hat, frowning at the large, expensive carriage parked outside the Halsey barn. "I needed to talk with the Captain. I should've sent word." His gaze pierced her from under the brim of his hat. "I didn't know you were expecting guests."

She tipped forward to untie her shoe, huffing at her impossibly stiff corset. "Mr. Haggerty's arrival was a surprise. We didn't expect him this soon."

The stable master's dog sniffed a carriage wheel. Head basking in the sun, he lifted a hind leg and gave the wheel a dousing. Jonas chuckled at the sight.

"But you *did* expect him."

She tried again to bend low. "He is betrothed to me. A fact that didn't seem to bother you last night."

His mouth flattened in a grim line. She fussed with the bottom of her stomacher where a stay dug deep into the side of her waist. The corset, like the gown, was made for a youthful woman. The whalebone's pinch and her ugly gown reminded her, she was twenty-four, not a young girl anymore. Life had changed and she needed to change with it, otherwise the things she wanted—a husband, children, to write a few Romanesque adventures—would all go up in smoke.

Like it or not, her best chance at what she wanted was inside her drawing room. Mr. Haggerty had made it clear what he wanted. Jonas had not.

She tried again to bend forward. "This blasted corset."

"Here. Let me." Jonas knelt before her and nudged her hem a discreet fraction. He was going to untie her shoes.

It was silly, watching him intently, his long, tanned fingers hooking the back of her shoe as he set the fripperies one at a time on the bench beside her. Wintry air nipped her. Toes curling, she started to hide them under her hem.

Big, warm hands wrapped around her silk-clad foot. Her arch tingled. A callused finger stroked a line from her ankle under her heel along her arch to the balls of her feet. The snagging sounds seduced her better than pretty words. She swallowed hard...last night's passion. With fumbling hands, she raised her hood as if the cloth gave the privacy she craved with Jonas. He tucked her foot into one boot and took his time pulling up the leather.

His thumbs slid slowly up her calf.

"Jonas," she whispered, glancing around the yard. At least they were alone.

Wide shoulders rose and fell with his measured breathing. Head bent and hat on, she couldn't see his face, but he knew the impropriety of a man's hands lingering under a woman's hem. This was agony. To feel his warmth. To smell him and the spicy-scented soap he'd used to shave. Fisting in her cloak, she dare not touch him. If she did, they'd kiss. Full. Hot. Unguarded.

Jonas sought the second boot. His fingers dug into the leather. Would Mr. Haggerty with his grand plans to dress her be this affected? Her mouth clamped painfully. There was much to adore about Jonas and his silent strength, but even the best of men had to bare their hearts. Would Jonas count her worthy of the risk?

He tucked the second boot past her ankle, going faster. Officious hands left off with the leather half up her calf. "I expect to finish the chair in the next few days." His voice was taut.

"That will be helpful."

Jonas brushed her hem down and pushed off the ground. Hands clamped behind his back, he eyed the tower. His neck turned beet red, the color climbing up his cheeks. "About my conversation with the Captain…"

"Yes?" She rose from the bench, jamming her heel into the second boot.

The fit was awkward but they began their stroll to the tower, passing the kitchen garden with its rows of upturned soil. Chickens scratched through the snow, their beaks pecking the ground. She pulled the keys from her pocket and kept a respectable arm's-length from Jonas.

"You know I came to settle things with the Captain," he intoned. "It's why I came back to Plumtree."

Sunlight hurt her eyes, its blinding brightness bouncing off melting snow. She tugged her hood forward to shade her eyes. "Yes. To make your peace with him about the fire and your hasty departure."

"And for being a neglectful grandson." His baritone voice rumbled comfortingly at her side. "You, however, have been a fine example of family duty."

They took a side path to the tower, but the manor's back edifice was in full view. So, too, was the drawing room's glass doors where Mr. Haggerty kept watch. Waving, she attempted a smile but her lips stuck to her gums. Mr. Haggerty scowled, giving her a curt nod.

"We do what we must," she said, facing the tower again.

"Which brings me to you."

"Me?"

"As I said, you are a shining example of family honor and responsibility."

"Don't you mean a liar? This past year I've managed to deceive my father's publisher and his antiquarian friends. And though I've not said marriage vows, I feel like I've cuckolded the man standing in my mother's drawing room. I could allow myself those first sins because they help my family. But the last? It was all for me."

Muddy snow sucked her boots. Misery was a stone in the pit of her stomach. Had she mucked up her future for an unwise tumble? The corset banded her ribs in a painful grip and the skin between her legs was sore. Jonas would soon put Plumtree behind him. No, Jonas would soon put her behind him. It had to be the reason for his stiff gait and lack of eye contact. He was ready to run off the same as he did ten years ago.

But, this time he'd not come back.

They walked into the tower's shadow, the sun's loss chilling her. She fussed with her skirts, trying to save her hems. It was daft since she wished the gown gone forever.

"For me, too," he said.

Her head snapped up. "What?"

"Last night was..." Words trailing, Jonas squinted at nothing in particular.

She leaned in. "Yes?"

The toes of her boots pushed deeper in the earth. Her heart expanded as if it climbed into her throat. She couldn't swallow. She didn't breathe. She teetered, waiting, hoping.

"I want to do what's right. I'll follow your excellent example and do my best for the Captain." Hands firmly behind his back and feet spread wide, Jonas spewed words. "I think we should, that is, considering what happened last night, we ought to come to an arrangement ourselves. You are a fine woman. My income cannot rival what you've enjoyed. I established a decent annuity from my work with the earl...that and re-establishing Braithwaite Furniture should count as worthy for your consideration. We'll muddle through."

"Muddle through?"

Jonas's little speech had all the ardor of a limp vegetable. Who was this man standing before her with all his talk of family responsibility and income? Mrs. Bainbridge's words of wisdom blended with her mother's. An arrangement with a man was cold comfort. Jonas was doing his duty and giving her the promise of a comfortable life.

He wasn't giving her his heart.

She opened the tower door. Her limbs numbed as if she'd slept oddly on them. Nothing worked properly, certainly not the man in front of her. Jonas tugged his cravat as if it were Tyburn's noose.

No! No! No!

This wasn't happening.

The back doors of the drawing room opened. Mr. Haggerty stepped outside, facing the tower and shading his eyes. In a way, the man waiting for her by the drawing room was willing to give her more than her friend of many years. It was heart-aching. Demoralizing.

"Thank you for your kind offer, but I cannot accept." She faced Jonas, pained to the soles of her feet.

His jaw dropped. "Livvy?"

Jonas blanched. The blankness in his eyes searching her...he was empty. Hollow.

The numbness faded, replaced by discomfort. Everywhere. Her stomach churned. She wanted to cast up her accounts. Hand on her midsection, she pressed her stomacher.

"You don't have to work on the chair," she mumbled.

"Bugger the chair." He took a step toward her and stopped when she took a step back.

Clarity was bright as the blinding winter sun. She knew what she wanted and she'd not settle for anything less.

"All these years, I didn't know what I've been waiting for. But now I do," she said, her voice growing steadier with each word. "It was you. Not some business arrangement or a man to choose me out of a sense of *duty* and *responsibility*. It was you I've wanted."

Head shaking and arms spread wide, he said, "I cannot be more here than this."

Jonas glowered at her, his black brows snapping in a fierce show of emotion. At least he showed anger well. She'd take it if it meant getting the rest of him. All of him. It was his love, his heart she wanted.

"I don't know what else to do, what else to give." His arms flopped to his sides.

Her fist clenched on her breast bone, a tremor edging her voice. "There's only one thing I want from you, but you...I..."

She searched his eyes unable to finish. Then, quietly, proudly, she walked away.

Chapter Ten

JONAS TOSSED HIS laundry into the sea chest. Cambric shirts tangled with neck cloths which twined with stockings and breeches. He kicked the chest against the wall. It slid across the floor and banged into the wall supporting the window, the same window Livvy Halsey had climbed in and out of his bedchamber.

"Bloody sea chest," he mumbled and lifted the lid.

"Bad day at the Halseys?" The Captain shuffled inside and his rump dropped into the winged chair by the fire.

"No."

"Want to tell me about it?"

"No."

Jonas rearranged the clothes, but it was all for naught. He added more chaos than order. From his crouch in front of the sea chest, he took a good look at the Captain. The lines on the old man's face, the snowy hair peeking out of his night cap, the spindly ankles above his shoes. His grandfather sniffed and dabbed a handkerchief to his nose. He nursed his annual winter ailment, a mild fever with the sniffles. It came every winter when Jonas was a boy. The Captain would wear his banyan and nurse himself with beef tea, spending a day or two abed.

Holding on to the sea chest, Jonas's heart cracked. His grandfather had been his rock, but the Captain, who was always old, was getting older. The finality of it hit him in the same place on his chest where Livvy had fisted her hand on her breast bone. Life's threads were fragile.

Apparently, the thread between him and Livvy Halsey was fragile, too. He'd believed differently. Facing her had scared him, so too had her rejection. Emotion slid like quicksilver through his veins. His blood boiled worse than when he faced down real pirates.

"I always thought she was allowed too much freedom." The Captain chuckled, settling in the chair. "A continental mother...what else can one expect?"

"Mrs. Halsey is a fine woman with a kind heart." Jonas picked up the empty leather pouch that once held the watch. "So is Livvy."

"Indeed. But one can only assume the disaster that comes from letting a girl have that much independence and book learning. Not to mention all that digging in the dirt she did with her father." The Captain shivered visibly. "Disastrous."

Jonas tucked the leather back in the sea chest. "Or it makes for a fascinating woman."

"She's a woman who wants her way."

"Because she's certain about *what* she wants. It's refreshing." His shoulders squared with a sense of purpose. Yes, Livvy knew what she wanted and she was not going to settle for anything less.

And she wanted his heart. Bared to him. Open. Honest. Ready to give and receive.

"Didn't seem refreshing when you stormed in an hour ago," the Captain said sagely.

He shut the sea chest. "Because I was angry."

"And you solved your anger by stomping off?"

"No, she did."

"If there's one thing I've learned," the Captain said, raising a bony finger to the ceiling. "With women, a man must try and try again until he gets it right."

"What is the *it* in your wisdom, sir?"

The old man shrugged. "Understanding mystery of a woman. The right woman, the kind who makes a man move heaven and earth to have her because he will be miserable for the rest of his days if she is not by his side. That's the *it* I mean."

Jonas removed his earring and stared at the gold piece in his palm. He had crossed oceans, thinking of Livvy. He would cross them again if it meant reaching this ephemeral understanding. Slipping the gold onto his finger, it went past the first knuckle. Perhaps it wasn't all that difficult. He didn't have to cross an ocean. He had to cross a meadow and this time give Livvy what she wanted.

It was him. All of him. Even the parts he was scared to show.

"What are you going to do m'boy?"

"I'm going to try again. This time, I'll get it right." Jonas exited the room. From the corner of his eye, he caught the Captain's fists clenched high in victory.

"THE CARVING IS amazingly intact," Mr. Kendall said in awe.

Livvy wrapped her shawl tightly about, her breath fogging the tower window. True to form, Mr. Kendall insisted on seeing all items to be catalogued in the marital contract, especially the curule chair.

The rule of not allowing others into the tower was set aside.

Livvy stared out the mullioned window as lifeless and empty as she'd been since leaving Jonas at the tower door. The world of valuations and assets could hang. Her heart was broken. Pain stole her wish for conversation, and Mr. Haggerty thoughtfully left her alone. She'd tossed the blanket high up on the tower bed, but her betrothed saw the maneuver. His eyes flashed blackly and he stalked off to examine the broken gladius and breast plate, letting her stew while her mother and Mr. Kendall haggled over earthly goods.

There were more worthy things to discuss. Love or the lack of it.

But no one brought up *that* marital asset.

Livvy traced a circle in the foggy glass. This was not an auspicious beginning to her soon-to-be marriage.

Drawing in the glass, she spied a dark figure running through the meadow. She dragged her palm over the mullioned panes. Jonas? Snow kicked up behind him. His long legs ate up the ground as if the devil nipped his heels.

She unlatched the window. "Jonas?"

"Livvy!" He ran faster to the tower, his black coat flaring like a cape behind him until he was under her window. Jonas dropped down on both knees. He took off his hat and set it over his heart. "Livvy."

There was a commotion behind her. Heels slamming the floor, voices, but she planted both hands wide on the windowsill and blocked them out.

"Is something wrong? Is the Captain in good health?"

"The Captain is well," he said, panting from his sprint. "But, I am not."

"What?" She leaned out at the waist.

"Livvy, I made a mess of things with you. I wasn't entirely truthful."

"What the devil is going on here?" Good Mr. Kendall tried to muscle his way to a spot at the window, but Mr. Haggerty grabbed his arm.

"Go on," she said, facing out the window again.

Jonas pulled something off his forefinger and held it high between thumb and forefinger. Sunlight glinted on gold.

"It's my earring. I told you and your mother only part of the story."

"Why the devil does anyone care about the man's earring?" Mr. Kendall said behind her.

"Mr. Kendall, please." Her mother's voice was at her shoulder. "I want to hear this."

"The day I got the earring, I was waiting with the other sailors, but I was lonely. Sad." His arms spread wide, hanging there a second before flopping to his sides. "I didn't want to die alone. I wanted to be with people who meant a great deal to me. People like...you."

Her breath caught. "Yes."

"When it was my turn, I laid my head on the piercer's table. He put a chunk of wood between my neck and earlobe. Just before he drove the needle into my ear he said something that changed everything. Something that made me decide to return to England...to return to you."

"What was it?" her mother whispered at Livvy's back.

"He warned me there would be pain." Jonas smiled as if the weight of the world had come off his shoulders. "And then he said, 'Think of what makes you happy'."

"And?" Livvy's hand balled tightly on her breastbone.

"I thought of you."

Air gusted from her. Emotions twined, soft and endearing for the man pouring out his heart to her.

"I thought of years of laughing with you, of wading in the River Trent, and you speaking your mind and me listening. And I wanted more. I wanted the rest of my life to be that and more with you, because I love you, Livvy Halsey. I think I always have."

"Oh, Jonas! Stay right there!" She tore across the room and sped down the stairs, her plain, leather shoes beating a staccato rhythm.

Outside the tower, she tromped through muddy snow, splashing her skirts. Jonas waited for her, both knees in the snow. She tackled him and showered his face with kisses as they rolled in the snow.

"I love you, Jonas," she cried between kisses. Tears began to flow, wetting her cheeks and his. "I will marry you."

"A tale of a painful ear-piercing?" Mr. Kendall's voice carried from the tower. "That has to be the worst marriage proposal I have ever had the displeasure of hearing."

"I think it's wonderful," her mother said, her voice joyful.

Jonas wrapped his arms and the ends of his coat around her, keeping his back in the snow. He kissed her tears and her cheeks. From her side vision, she spied Mr. Haggerty looking out the window, an odd half-smile on his face as she hugged Jonas.

Livvy couldn't be sure, but she thought he said something about, "…this is a good time to renegotiate the price of the curule chair…"

She took the gold earring and slipped it on her finger. "I'll wear this ring forever. Because whatever we do, whatever adventures are to be had, we are in this life together."

Jonas caressed her cheek. In the tender touch was a promise of forever. "Always together, Livvy." Slow and sweet, he kissed her, finishing with a whisper against her lips, "Always."

THE END

ABOUT THE AUTHOR

Gina Conkle writes lush Viking romance and sensual Georgian romance. Her books always offer a fresh, addictive spin on the genre, with the witty banter and sexual tension that readers crave. She grew up in southern California and despite all that sunshine, Gina loves books over beaches and stone castles over sand castles. Now she lives in Michigan with her favorite alpha male, Brian, and their two sons where she's known to occasionally garden and cook.

Find out more about her books at ginaconkle.com or join her newsletter for free reads and book news.

Midnight Meetings series
Meet the Earl at Midnight, book 1
The Lady Meets Her Match, book 2
The Lord Meets His Lady, book 3
Meet a Rogue at Midnight, book 4

CPSIA information can be obtained
at www.ICGtesting.com
Printed in the USA
LVOW10s0054291117
557961LV00008B/244/P

9 781976 345227